D0153139

American Indian Literature
and Critical Studies Series

Gerald Vizenor, General Editor

ONLY APPROVED INDIANS
Stories

Apache, Navaho, and Spaniard (Norman, 1960, 1994; Westport, Conn., 1980)

(ed.) *The Indian in America's Past* (Englewood Cliffs, 1964)

Warriors of the Colorado: The Yumas of the Quechan Nation and Their Neighbors (Norman, 1965)

Afro-Americans in the Far West (Berkeley, 1967)

(ed.) *Nevada Indians Speak* (Reno, 1967)

Native Americans of California and Nevada (Healdsburg, 1969, 1982)

(ed.) *Aztecas del Norte: The Chicanos of Aztlán* (New York, 1973)

American Words: An Introduction to Those Native Words Used in English (Davis, Calif., 1979)

Native Americans and Nixon: Presidential Policy and Minority Self-Determination (Los Angeles, 1982)

(ed.) *Native American Higher Education: The Struggle for the Creation of D-Q University* (Davis, Calif., 1985)

Black Africans and Native Americans: Race, Caste and Color in the Evolution of Red-Black Peoples (Oxford, 1988; Urbana, 1933, as *Africans and Native Americans*)

Columbus and Other Cannibals: The Wétiko Disease of Exploitation, Imperialism, and Terrorism (New York, 1992)

ONLY APPROVED INDIANS

Stories
by Jack D. Forbes

UNIVERSITY OF OKLAHOMA PRESS
NORMAN AND LONDON

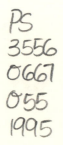

PS
3556
O667
O55
1995

Library of Congress Cataloging-in-Publication Data

Forbes, Jack D.
    Only approved Indians: stories / by Jack D. Forbes
        p. cm. — (American Indian literature and critical studies
series: v. 12)
        ISBN 0-8061-2699-X (acid-free paper)
        1. Indians of North America—Social life and customs—
Fiction.
    I. Title. II. Series
    PS3556.0667055 1995
    813'.54—dc20   94-24338
                                                                      CIP

The paper in this book meets the guidelines for permanence and
durability of the Committee on Production Guidelines for Book
Longevity of the Council on Library Resources, Inc. ∞

Only Approved Indians: Stories, is Volume 12 in the AMERICAN
INDIAN LITERATURE AND CRITICAL STUDIES SERIES.

1   2   3   4   5   6   7   8   9   10

Dedicated to my wife,
Carolyn L. Forbes
(Go na shá Se ka náy)

CONTENTS

PREFACE AND ACKNOWLEDGMENTS

I WROTE MY FIRST SHORT STORY WHEN I WAS A YOUNG student at Glendale College. It was a true story, but the instructor gave it a "B" because it was "unbelievable." Almost thirty years later I started writing short fiction again.

"Only Approved Indians Can Play Made in USA," my first 1979 story, was published in Simon J. Ortiz's anthology, *Earth Power Coming: Short Fiction in Native American Literature* (Tsaile, Arizona: Navajo Community College Press, 1984), and in Wesley Brown and Amy Ling's *Imagining America: Stories from the Promised Land* (New York: Persea Books, 1991). This story also appeared in Sylvan Barnett (ed.), *An Introduction to Literature* (New York: HarperCollins, 1994).

My first published short story was "The Professor," which appeared in *Winds of Change* (a local Yolo County newspaper) 2(8) (March 1981); 14. The second was "The Caged," published in *Winds of Change* (June 1981: 6–7) and *Okike: An African Journal of New Writing,* no. 19 (September 1981); 54–61, and reprinted in *Critical Perspectives of Third World America* 1(1) (Fall 1983); 56–64. "South of Hope" appeared in *Winds of Change* 4 (4) (April 1983); 15, and in *Rikka* (Canada) 9(1) (Spring 1984); 38–40.

Of the other stories, "A City Indian Goes to School" was written in 1979; "The Laying On of the Hands," "The Cave," "Shaw," "When Professors Die," "Southside," and "The Sacrifice" were all written in 1980, more or less in that order. "An Incident in a Tour Among the Natives," probably written in England after May 1982, appeared in *Rikka* 12(1) (1987); 31–33. "My Father's Visit" was put to pen in 1982, also in England. "The Edge of Things" was written shortly thereafter back in the United States, whereas "South of Hope" was put to pen in early 1983. "Someone to Love" came to me a little later. "Lendra" was written in Leiden and Rotterdam in 1984.

"The Laying On of the Hands" was published in Russian in Alexandr Vaschenko's *In Nature's Heartbeat: Literature of Native Americans and Native Siberians*, vol. 2 (Moscow: Lantin, 1992), whereas "The Cave" was anthologized in Clifford Earl Trafzer (ed.), *Earth Song* (New York: Doubleday, 1993). "The Dream of Injun Joe" was included in *Gone to Croatan*, edited by James Koehnline and Ron Sakolsky (Brooklyn: Autonomedia, 1993). "When Professors Die" appeared in *Gatherings* 3 (Fall 1992); 82–85. "The Edge of Things" was published in a special issue of *Callaloo* (January-February 1994); 325–33.

I wish to thank the many persons who have critiqued or read some or all of these stories, including Carolyn Forbes, Sarah Hutchison, Carmen Mays, Annette Reed-Crum, Lorna Brown, A.S.C.A. Muijen, Traci Gourdine, and Christoph Burkard. I also want to thank Huell Hutchison and Kelly Crabtree for their help in the final preparation of the manuscript. Finally, I want to thank everyone else who provided me with feedback or helped with typing.

The characters in these stories are fictional. Any relationship to living persons is purely coincidental.

JACK D. FORBES

ONLY APPROVED INDIANS
Stories

ONLY APPROVED INDIANS CAN PLAY MADE IN USA

THE ALL-INDIAN BASKETBALL TOURNAMENT WAS IN ITS second day. Excitement was pretty high, because a lot of the teams were very good, or at least eager and hungry to win. Quite a few people had come out to watch, mostly Indians. Many were relatives or friends of the players. A lot of people were betting money and tension was pretty great.

A team from the Tucson Inter-Tribal House was set to play against a group from the Great Lakes region. The Tucson players were mostly very dark young men, with long black hair. A few had goatees or mustaches, though, and one of the Great Lakes fans had started a rumor that they were really Chicanos. This was a big issue since the Indian Sports League had a rule that all players had to be of one-quarter or more Indian blood and that they had to have their BIA roll numbers available if challenged.

And so a big argument started. One of the biggest, darkest Indians on the Tucson team had been singled out as a Chicano, and the crowd wanted him thrown out. The Great Lakes players, most of whom were pretty light, refused to start. They all had their BIA identification cards, encased in plastic. This proved that they were all real Indians, even a blonde-haired guy. He was really only about one-sixteenth, but the BIA rolls had been changed for his tribe, so legally he was one-fourth. There was no question about the Great Lakes team. They were all land-based, federally-recognized

Indians (although living in a big midwestern city), and they had their cards to prove it.

Anyway, the big, dark Tucson Indian turned out to be a Papago. He didn't have a BIA card, but he could talk Papago, so they let him alone for the time being. Then they turned toward a lean, very Indian-looking guy who had a pretty big goatee. He seemed to have a Spanish accent, so they demanded to see his card.

Well, he didn't have one either. He said that he was a full-blood Tarahumara Indian and that he could also speak his language. None of the Great Lakes Indians could talk their languages, so they said that was no proof of anything, that you had to have a BIA roll number.

The Tarahumara man was getting pretty angry by then. He said his father and uncle had been killed by the whites in Mexico and that he did not expect to be treated with prejudice by other Indians.

But all that did no good. Someone demanded to know if he had a reservation and if his tribe was recognized. He replied that his people lived high up in the mountains and that they were still resisting the Mexicanos, that the government was trying to steal their land.

"What state do your people live in?" they wanted to know. When he said that his people lived free, outside of the control of any state, they only shook their fists at him. "You're not an official Indian. All official Indians are under the white man's rule now. We all have a number given to us to show that we are recognized."

Well, it all came to an end when someone shouted, "Tarahumaras don't exist. They're not listed in the BIA dictionary." Another fan yelled, "He's a Mexican. He can't play. This tournament is only for Indians."

The officials of the tournament had been huddling

together. One blew a whistle, and an announcement was made: "The Tucson team is disqualified. One of its members is a Yaqui. One is a Tarahumara. The rest are Papagos. None of them have BIA enrollment cards. They are not Indians within the meaning of the laws of the government of the United States. The Great Lakes team is declared the winner by default."

A tremendous roar of applause swept through the stands. A white BIA official wiped the tears from his eyes and said to a companion, "God bless America. I think we've won."

THE CAGED

THE TIME HE LOOKED FORWARD TO SO MUCH HAD JUST about arrived. Already the crowds had thinned out and only a few people stopped to look at him. Soon the loudspeaker would blare out its message and the last visitors would scurry toward the gates.

There was something about closing time that he could understand very well. The last onlookers seemed anxious to leave as soon as closing time was announced. They were afraid, it seemed, of being caught in the Garden of Science after dark, afraid that at night, in some strange way, all of the caged creatures might break their bars and prowl loose, tearing the visitors to pieces or even eating them.

But closing time, while it promised relief, was always a dangerous time. At that hour, when the crowds had thinned and the guards were relaxing, young boys, sometimes encouraged by adults, would hurl things into the cages. Often it was just trash, but sometimes they threw rocks or pieces of cement. Their object, as he well knew, was to provoke the captives into uncontrolled rage or simply to inflict pain and cause them to scream out.

But Lo had learned long ago to control his rage. After many years of incarceration he had cultivated an appearance of utter indifference to his obscene tormenters, whatever their form of torture. When he did choose to react, it was only in extreme cases, and for those he had devised a suitable counterattack.

Lo was supposed to relieve himself in a little hole in the floor partially shielded from the onlookers' stares. But he usually managed to hide some excrement in a place where the attendants wouldn't notice. Then, when provoked to the extreme, he would rapidly grasp handfuls of feces and hurl them in the faces of his tormenters, following that up with pieces of cement or whatever was at hand. He would then shake the bars and roar, and quite generally, the people outside would flee.

Of course, the attendants would then usually come with a powerful water hose or with electric prods, but he was used to such punishment. Even while being hosed down, he felt a certain satisfaction, for, if only for a few minutes, he had the sense of being a free creature, free to give vent to the desire for revenge, free to strike back.

For Lo the period after dark, when the Garden was quiet and peaceful, was the best part of the day. Sometimes he crouched next to the bars and watched the moon or the stars for hours. He often sat with both arms stretched out between the steel, as far as they could extend, so that he could feel the air out there. It was a different texture of air, it seemed, outside of the cage. Sometimes he would work his feet through the bars as well to allow the breeze to brush against his limbs. And he often inhaled so very hard to catch the fragrance of blossoms or wet grass or wood smoke. Once in a long while he could smell the ocean on the breeze, or the aroma of a river, but perhaps that was only his imagination.

Lo lived in his dreams a great deal of the time. He tried not to let memories from the daylight hours interfere with his nighttime freedom. He had disciplined himself to reserve the darkness for himself only, not allowing the people outside to dominate him totally.

During the day he succeeded in ignoring them most of the time, but this was always something of an effort. He didn't want that same feeling at night.

Occasionally his thoughts turned to Princess. He hadn't seen her for ages, maybe for a year or two. He didn't like to think of her at night because such thoughts inevitably disturbed him, made him melancholy and restless and then angry and bitter.

But sometimes he couldn't help it.

She had been so pretty, not that she was beautiful as such, but pretty in a way that he couldn't pin down. When they had brought her to his cage, she had been very frightened. They had put a little skirt on her, but otherwise she was unclothed, and he had noticed her breasts right away.

The guards prodded her into Lo's cage. He knew what they wanted him to do. Outside were a whole crowd of scientists in white coats or suits and ties, and some wealthy sponsors of the Gardens. They were all there to see him mate with Princess. Lo knew that.

He watched their faces, feeling only hate as he read their expressions. Some were smiling knowingly; others had their mouths opened wide in unabashed expectation.

Lo knew what they wanted, but he also knew that he would never accommodate them.

He moved over to one side of his cage and just sat there passively. He ignored Princess. She gradually calmed down as she realized that he was not going to rush at her, but the scientists became upset. They started trying to coax him but ended yelling obscenities.

Every day was the same. They took Princess away at night so he could never be alone with her. They had cameras ready to take pictures of the mating, but Lo always refused to cooperate.

The scientists finally set up hidden cameras and left Princess for a while at night, but she and Lo kept apart. They both knew and understood. They wanted to touch and to love each other, but they knew, they understood, and they refused.

Finally, the scientists showed them a film of different creatures having intercourse, but Lo just turned his back and farted at them. A male scientist and a female one even made love to each other, just outside of the cage, so that Lo and Princess could learn, but Lo threw water at them and drove them away.

He knew very well what they wanted. They wanted to study a pregnancy and the birth of a baby. They wanted a new baby born in captivity. They wanted to keep a rare species from disappearing. Lo knew all of that.

But he wanted his species to disappear. He didn't want any children of his to have to grow up behind bars, in a cage, being studied by probing, curious, glassy-eyed people.

Finally they took Princess away. He had managed to gesture to her and even to whisper once, and she knew how he felt, even though he had never touched her physically. They understood each other, and they understood the ones outside as well.

Lo scratched himself and adjusted his breechcloth. All they ever gave him to wear, except in the winter, was a little piece of cloth, but sometimes, on special occasions, he had a blanket to sleep on and could drape that over his shoulders.

After many years he had come to understand the outsiders very well. He studied them closely and learned their words. He spoke them to himself often so as to while away the time. But they never knew.

To them he was completely stoic and unresponsive. He stared past them into space. Except when tormented, he refused to make any kind of contact with them.

But he listened. He heard what they had to say, especially if they remarked on something that might help him understand himself better.

One day a child had read out loud from a sign outside his cage. He had listened intently:

> Mister Lo: the last full-blood male American Indian known to be alive. It was long believed that no Indian had survived the Final Solution, but fortunately for science, Mister Lo was captured and brought here to the Garden of Science.
>
> American Indians are believed to have been distantly related to the primitive ancestors of other humanoid groups. Incapable of being civilized, they were eliminated by the process of evolution and the science of population eugenics.

Little by little he had put things together. Bits of conversation here, idle chatter by the guards, and lengthy observations by learned scientists had allowed him to reconstruct what had happened to his people, to others like himself. But still, there was much that he didn't know.

Of his life before captivity he could remember very little. He had been quite young and living alone. He had only vague memories of being with other people like himself. Still, he had not forgotten that once upon a time no bars had surrounded him.

Sometimes, for a too-short while, the moonlight streamed directly into my cage. I liked to bask in it, although it gave no warmth. Often, though, after a moon-bath I felt like dreaming and my thoughts wandered back perhaps to my childhood, or to some previous life. In such moments I was in the mountains, usually along a stream, with no bars around. It was beautiful and I lovingly touched the plants, the grass, the rocks. I smelled food cooking and watched a woman, my mother, at the fire.

I never allowed white people into my dreams. They came in only at the very end, and I always stopped and woke up at that point.

In the cage, of course, I had nothing but time. So as the years went by I learned to gradually control my dreams, to use them as a means of understanding. I had to try to remember everything, to rebuild what the tortures had driven from my mind. Eventually I realized that I would have to allow whites into my dreams in order to comprehend what had happened, but I only did that during the day when I couldn't be by myself anyway.

The outsiders thought I was just sleeping or staring past them into space or pacing for exercise. Sometimes as I became agitated by a memory, I would walk endlessly back and forth, as in a trance, or rock on my heels. In this way my agitated inner life was revealed in my external behavior but in such a way as to mislead my tormenters.

I lived again through the days of torture. After I was first captured the people in white coats, whom I later learned to call scientists, experimented endlessly with me. I was often fastened and could not move. They filled me with drugs, they forced me to eat, they made me inhale marijuana smoke, they masturbated my penis and measured its length, they made me listen to different kinds of sounds, they surrounded me with different kinds of colors.

Much of what they were saying I didn't understand until later. It seems that I was caged up in what they called a university and that students planning to be scientists were writing articles about me. They called me a "guinea pig" for a long time, until they gave me the name of "Lo the Poor Indian," and finally just "Mister Lo."

While I was in the university a girl scientist tried to

tame me. She was nice to me, gave me treats, and touched me softly. She spoke gently and smiled a lot. She tried to teach me her language, and at first I looked forward to her being there with me.

Eventually they thought I was tamed down enough and she took me on walks, although I was still hobbled at the ankles and my hands were tied. It was such a relief to get away from the torture experiments that I was just like a pet dog. I did everything she wanted me to do; that is, until I saw one time that she was taking notes on me just like all the rest. Then I caught her laughing once, and I knew she had tricked me. The next time she came near I spat in her face and kicked her with both my feet.

Every time I didn't do what they wanted, they gave me electric shocks. Eventually, though, they grew tired of studying me and I was taken to the zoo, what they call the Garden of Science, for exhibition.

Anyhow, all of the terrible things those scientists did almost drove me crazy. I wiped it all out afterward, along with the memory of my early life. But in order to remember the past I have had to force myself to recall, day by day, everything that has happened since my capture.

What I came to realize is this: if a creature learns to completely accept captivity or slavery, if they erase all thoughts of freedom, they can suppress the pain. But if one wants to be free, one has to face the pain; one has to agonize, to suffer, through all of the terror. One has to face up to what has happened, to face up to one's complete degradation.

They wanted me to become a happy little prisoner, pleasing the crowds and loving my captors. I could have done that if I had accepted their definition of what I was or if I had accepted the pet dog role in order to avoid pain. But once I came to realize what they had done to my race, to my relatives, to my family, I was no longer afraid of the pain. I wanted to share the suffering my people had suffered.

So it was that, little by little, I rediscovered my own soul and memory while at the same time making them believe that I was only dull-witted and indifferent to everything.

One thing that helped me was this: every so often people came to look at me who didn't joke or throw popcorn. They were sad-eyed and seemed ashamed. Sometimes they spoke quietly to each other and said things that I interpreted as expressing sympathy. I got the impression that most of them had some Indian blood but that they were white in their way of life.

One young man of that type had a special effect on me. He had very large, sad eyes set in a face that would have been attractive if it had not been disfigured by a scar on one cheek, a scar that pulled his face out of shape. One of his arms was also damaged in some way and he walked with a slight limp.

He came to see me when very few other people were around and he seemed to sort of talk to himself. I learned later that he was praying for me.

After many visits he began to lean close to the cage and to talk to me. He said things like, "My name is Ben. I want to be your friend. I'm not going to call you Lo. I will call you Eagle Flying because I want your spirit to fly free, like an eagle up in the sky."

Then he would point up to the sky. He would repeat all that he said and would point to objects to teach me the meaning of his words. I gradually took a friendly interest in him, but out of deep distrust of all outsiders I said nothing. One day he said, "Deep inside of all of us is a thing we cannot see. It is our spirit and that spirit is part of a greater spirit-power that we call the Great Spirit. Each of us is like a drop of water and the Great Spirit is like the ocean.

"You must have hope. Your spirit cannot really be destroyed by them. They can torture and abuse you, but your spirit cannot be touched. It only goes into hiding. It is beyond their reach.

"We are all children of the Great Spirit. So we call it Grandfather. We talk with our Grandfather even though He is inside of us, even as He is also outside and everywhere.

"I will teach you a prayer. It goes, 'Grandfather, Great Spirit, hear my voice. Help me, Grandfather. Help all living creatures. Help all those who suffer. Help all my relations. Thank you, Grandfather.'

"Now you listen to those words and try to repeat them. Someday you can say them to yourself."

Then he gave me a beautiful blue stone. He threw it to me and I picked it up. I wanted to cry. Tears came to my eyes, but I could not cry there in that cage. But he saw the tears.

The very next time he came, after he had been praying for a time I spoke to him.

"Ben . . . you are my only friend. I thank you."

My voice sounded very strange to me. It must have sounded even more strange to Ben! For a long time he could only stare at me, but eventually a smile brightened up his face and he clasped his hands together in glee.

Just then other people came and he left, but later we talked again. I said, "I have learned how to talk this language, my friend. Now we can speak to each other, since I trust you. The Great Spirit tells me that you are a good person, different from those who have tortured me."

"Eagle Flying, you should know that I and many others have been tortured by the same oppressors. How do you think I got to be the way I am? They used me for medical experiments and almost killed me, because I did not obey them quickly enough and because I was overheard praying to the Great Spirit in the Indian way.

"I am half-Indian by blood, Eagle Flying, but my spirit is all Indian. Their tortures burned away forever all of the white flesh from me.

"So you are not alone!"

He told me that he would come back as often as possible and that other secret Indians would visit me also. I would know them by their pointing to the sky and saying, "Eagle Flying." He also warned me that I must not be impatient for their visits, because they had to be extremely cautious so as not to draw attention to themselves.

One time Ben said to me, "You should know that we do not hate all white people. You must realize that all people are watched and that all who deviate from the government's orders are turned over to the personality engineers for behavior modification, as they call it. This means that they are tortured repeatedly until they learn to obey all rules. Those who cannot correct their behavior are operated on by neurosurgeons and are turned into robots, or what we call zombies. These zombies always obey orders and do what they are told."

I asked him, "How can they control so many people this way? Don't they fight back?"

"Eagle Flying, many years ago the scientists were told to find ways to keep the people in line. They now use what they call positive and negative reinforcement. In other words, they reward people if they do what they are told and punish them if they disobey. Of course, the white people get the greatest rewards, while we mixed-bloods and the blacks get the greatest punishments. But that is another story.

"What they call science has triumphed, Eagle Flying, and as you well know, the people in the white coats can do whatever they wish in the name of what they call the search for knowledge so long as they do not experiment on the rulers. And, of course, the 'knowledge' they uncover is usually used to better control us.

"But do not look so sad. Some of us have managed to survive, with the help of our Grandfather. Do not give up hope, for hope is a powerful medicine from the Great Spirit. Don't let it go!"

And, indeed, I did not give up hope. In fact, hope began as a new emotion for me, since it meant now much more than just the desire for the cessation of pain.

I began to seriously hope for freedom from my cage. I began to pray, and finally I fasted to seek spiritual guidance. At first, I didn't dare fast for four days at a time, because I was afraid of becoming weak. But finally I was able to do even that. You, of course, are hearing my words now because of what happened after that sacrifice, but I am jumping ahead.

One night I was surprised by a low whisper near my cage. It was a moonless, dark night, but soon I recognized several of my friends. They had managed to steal a set of keys and soon, with great care, my cage was opened through the feeding corridor.

It may seem hard to believe, but as I left that familiar place I was struck by sheer terror. I was actually afraid to leave that prison! It had been my home for so long and the bars had seemed to protect me from the crowds of outsiders, so I was uneasy about going out into the open world.

Anyway, my companions pulled me along and together we made our way to the outside fence and escaped from the Garden of Science. They had clothes for me to put on and a hat for me to use to cover my long hair. After that everything was confusion as they led me through what seemed like a forest and then along strange streets. Eventually we reached the river I had often smelled, following it to an area of older houses, where I was taken inside.

My first weeks of freedom were not really very free, because I was constantly taken from place to place, but little by little I learned to breath easier and to adjust to the strange life around me. Finally we reached a lonely place in the mountains where the part-Indians had a secret place of worship, a ceremonial center.

The smell of the forest, the clean water of a little mountain stream, and the high cliffs nearby all helped me learn to cry again. Tears of joy came to my eyes and I sobbed without restraint for the first time that I could remember. And it was the beauty of Mother Earth, her sights, her smells, her sounds, that finally loosened my self-imposed control and brought me back to the days of my childhood.

What can I say? No words can tell you what I felt.

A few days later my joy was increased beyond all bounds when my friends brought Princess to me. They had rescued her also, from a zoo in a different part of the country. For the first time ever we reached out and touched each other.

AN INCIDENT IN A TOUR AMONG THE NATIVES

"I VERY MUCH ADMIRE YOUR BEING AN AUTHOR! AN American Indian writer! Really, it is so marvelous. And, I must say, you are a very inspiring speaker."

"Thanks. I appreciate your interest in our people."

"Tell me, William. May I call you William? Tell me, are there many other Red Indians like you? I mean, I would have always thought that Indians were, well . . . I don't like the word 'primitive' but, well, I mean rather unsophisticated and not at all Westernised. But you seem educated and, if I may say so, quite refined."

"There are all kinds of Indians, all kinds. And anyway I am very primitive and not nearly so sophisticated as I might seem to be."

"I didn't mean to hurt your feelings! How dreadful! Please don't be angry. Really, I want to absorb your ideas; they are *so* unique. I mean about authenticity and honesty and naturalness. You are quite right in picturing Europeans as being rather false and schizophrenic. And your analysis of our exploitative social systems is so telling! I was especially entranced by your rejection of both capitalism *and* Marxism as equally a lot of rubbish. I quite agree . . . but you must not think that all of us are lacking in a desire to change."

"I don't condemn all Europeans."

"Yes and I'm so glad of that. I wouldn't want you to be a fanatic. I do deplore fanaticism, don't you? I mean extremes are often rather distasteful."

"We Indians try to follow the middle way, the way of common sense."

"Really! I would have thought that *common* sense was not all that good, but perhaps you mean *natural*, as opposed to mere majority, opinion."

"Among Indians we give a lot of weight to what our people think. They aren't dumb, you know. They have good natural sense and we try to get unanimity if we can. We trust our people, but at the same time we're free, as individuals, to go our own way. So we don't have any problem with *common* sense."

"I see."

"We're a down-to-earth people. Not fancy. Just honest, brave, loyal, and great at whatever we do, ey."

"Oh, yes, I see. I am sure you are exaggerating, but still it must be true. I mean how could the noble savage ideal be so popular if there wasn't some basis for it? I'm afraid that we Europeans have lost all of the noble savagery. . . ."

"Leaving only savagery. . . ."

"Please! Don't be unkind. We are not *that* bad."

"Just kidding! Like I say, I don't condemn all Europeans, just what their colonial descendants are doing."

"It's rather noisy in here, don't you think? Come, let's go out on the terrace . . . unless, of course, you're afraid of being alone with me."

"You're a very attractive woman, but I'm not afraid of you."

"Other guests will be jealous of me for my audacity in keeping you all to myself, but I've never had such an opportunity before. I mean, one doesn't see many Red Indians in Britain and . . . frankly, one doesn't often see a young man so handsome and, well, I will say it, so exciting—yes, exciting as you."

"Exciting? That's a new idea. No one has ever called me exciting before, ey."

"Your hair is so smooth. I do believe I like braided hair on a man. Do you mind my touching it? Let me see, where were we? There are so many things I want to learn from you. . . . You may think I'm not serious, but I really do want to learn about your people."

"Well, that's what we're over here for—to help people understand what we're up against, to get our story across."

"You are such a courageous people. So brave really. Tell me, I'm very curious. Do you still carry off women? Capture them, I mean? That is something I'm curious about."

"Capture women?"

"Let me tell you something, very confidentially. I feel that I can speak honestly to you. I've often had dreams of being captured and carried off. . . ."

"By Rudolph Valentino."

"No, now you're laughing at me. Oh, your shoulders are broad. I can feel the tight muscles there. How do you maintain yourself in such excellent physical condition?"

"I like to chase antelopes."

"Really?"

"Yes, and buffalo, too. I catch them bare-handed and eat them raw."

"Oh, now I know you're joking! You're making fun of me . . . but I don't care. Really, I don't."

"Well, the truth is I just capture bears."

"Oh. . . . Well, have you ever caught a woman? I mean carried her off and ravished her, like in all of the stories I've read about white women being carried off."

"Ha, ha. Where do you get these ideas? Our women are too tough to be carried off, and we never rape white women. That's just a lot of propaganda—just a lot of lies."

"But you did capture white women!"

"Maybe so, but nobody had sex with them until they wanted to choose a man."

"Really, that surprises me . . . but I guess it's the *noble* thing to do then, isn't it? And you *are* noble red men. I'm convinced of that more than ever after talking with you."

"Look here, I'm not a noble red man. I'm just an ordinary Indian. And I don't carry off white women, although some have tried to carry me off!"

"Oh! You make it sound so vulgar. . . . And did they ravish you?"

"We don't talk about it that way. And, anyway, the truth is that I've been too busy for that. We've been traveling so much, from city to city."

"So you haven't collected any scalps on this expedition?"

"Scalps? Wow! You really do have a distorted view of us! The English taught us how to cut off heads for trophies and bring back scalps. They paid for *our* own scalps!"

"Oh, don't tell me about that! I'm sorry I mentioned it. I really want to know about what Indian people are actually like. The truth! . . . Tell me about Native American women, the squaws. Are they forced to walk behind the man?"

"Squaws? Hey, that's a word we don't like. It's an Indian word that just means 'women.' We just call them women. And they walk wherever they want to."

"Really? What do you think about women's liberation?"

"Our women are already liberated—always have been. They are sweet and gentle and strong and tough at the same time. They are free. They do what they want to do."

"I like that! European men are really quite sexist, you know. Are Indian women good lovers?"

"*All* Indians are good lovers. We are the world's greatest lovers!"

"You *are* bragging, I believe. I would have thought that blacks were more famous as lovers. And Italians!"

"Well, I read an article that said that blacks and Europeans were slow to get started because they need erotic dances and music to get them excited. Our music is not erotic at all but we're here, aren't we? We don't have any pornography or dirty films or anything like that. We don't need it."

"How really marvelous! I *am* so anxious to learn about Indian ways. . . . But I need a teacher."

"A teacher?"

"I want so badly to be natural and authentic, don't you see? But I have to learn."

"Oh, yeah."

"William, have you been to any of the topless beaches of Europe? But I would have thought that was old hat to you. I mean Indian women have always exposed their breasts, haven't they? But you see we European women are trying to become more natural again."

"Yes, I can see that. Your dress doesn't leave much to the imagination!"

"Oh, William, I will confess to you that I feel rather *daring* tonight. I *love* the feeling of exposing my breasts but—believe it or not—I'm basically reserved. Ordinarily, I'm not so bold . . . in public. . . . You do find me attractive though, don't you?"

"Well, uh, yes. You are a beautiful woman. No doubt about that. But you know, you're not natural. I mean, it's one thing for traditional women to have bare breasts or to bathe naked or to breast-feed their babies. They may be beautiful, but it's not done to excite men. The way Europeans do it, it's, well, it's conscious. It seems to me, it's done to get male interest going."

"And does it?"

"What?"

"Does it get your interest going?"

"Well, I'd be a liar if I said no. But it's not just the view. I mean your hands are pretty active, too. So I can't say which is the most effective."

"If I'm bothering you, I'll stop. I'll move way over here, out of reach. But honestly, I am a naturally touching person. You attract me and I can't help myself."

"What about your husband? Aren't you worried about him becoming upset?"

"Don't be silly, William. He has his own passions, or I should say perversions. But, no, I won't be cruel. Let me simply say that we have a mature relationship, a mature attitude."

"Uh, oh. There's George rounding everybody up. I guess we have to go now. We have another performance tomorrow."

"Do you have to go? I could motor you over in the morning. . . . Please stay. . . . I won't beg you, though."

"Well, I think I should go. We have to plan what we're going to do."

"I have an idea! I have a cozy little flat of my own. Here, I'll give you the address. Please come and visit me. You can stay as long as you like. And William, I am very interested in your writing. I have connections in the publishing world. Perhaps I can help you with your book."

"Well . . ."

"Here! Come and visit me. I want so much to help you secure the audience you deserve."

"Thanks."

"I will be there on Tuesday. This is the number. Please call or come by."

"Adios. It was a real pleasure. I'll see what I can do."

"Goodbye, William."

SHAW

SHE WAS CALLED SOUTH WOMAN, BECAUSE THE SOUTH-
ern breezes told of spring and good weather and
green grasses lying down before the wind, of flowers
in bloom and ripe berries along the creeks. Her name
in Indian was Shawanekwa, sometimes called Sha-
wana by her family, usually just known as Shaw by
her friends.

When people looked for her in those days, they
had to be very active. They couldn't just sit around in
the parlor waiting for her to sedately sit down beside
them. No, they would have to go out in the fields or
along country roads or fishing creeks where she spent
all of her time with her friend Son.

Son had another name, but it doesn't matter. He
was an only child like her, and ever since he had come
into this world he had been known simply as Son. He
was almost two years older than Shaw, but for a long
time they had been inseparable. Everybody always
knew they would be found together, and nobody
thought that odd at all.

Out in that part of the reservation families were
few and far between, the land being shallow-soiled
and a lot of it covered with scrawny oaks that didn't
even make good timber, just good hardwood ash for
making hominy.

So it was sort of natural that Shaw and Son became
playmates. Of course, most girls couldn't have kept up
with Son, since he was not your hang-around-the-house

boy. But Shaw was born with a fierce determination, it seems, to do whatever Son did.

As soon as she was able, she would follow him around wherever he went. At first he was inclined to leave her behind, but Shaw made such an effort to keep up that he just had to respect her. Sometimes he would get to a fishing spot and be there a while before she would show up, all scratched and bruised, hair all messed up, but ready to help him string his fish and look for grubs and worms.

And so they grew up as nearly constant companions, walking to the school bus together, walking home, riding horseback over the rolling hills, working stock together, even fighting alongside each other. Occasionally there was a strange boy at school foolish enough to object to Shaw's presence on the play-yard or fool enough to make some remark about Son hanging around with a girl.

Son was not a rough boy. He was slow to anger, but he was strong enough and when somebody threatened Shaw, he was like a bull seeing red. Nobody ever bothered Shaw or Son twice that way.

And Shaw knew how to fight, too. Son had shown her lots of tricks and she was strong anyway from doing everything Son did. She wasn't big for her age, deceptively slim in fact, but all her muscles had been shaped by activity and she wasn't at all afraid of bruises or falls.

The boys her own age never messed with Shaw, and Son took care of the older ones. Sometimes they did it together. But there was nothing self-conscious about it. It seemed so natural for them to be friends.

Shaw didn't like to wear dresses. A cowboy-cut shirt and jeans were what she preferred, just like Son. In the spring, though, the high school required the girls to wear dresses, even country girls, and Shaw was forced to obey. Often she hid a pair of jeans and an old shirt alongside the bus stop behind some bushes, and she changed her clothes just as soon as she got off of the bus, with Son watching out for any passersby.

Son didn't think much about all of that. He and Shaw had gone swimming together many times and he was aware that her body was different from his and that she was no longer a little girl. Still, he thought of her as a younger sister, and the significance of her filling out and growing up escaped him for a long while.

The subject didn't escape everybody, though. Son's parents sometimes got together with Shaw's and they talked about the two of them being together all the time, but, like Indians usually are inclined, they accepted it and left them alone.

Boys began to notice Shaw at school, though. She was a striking girl in some unusual way. She was pretty enough, with rich brown skin the color of wild honey and long black hair, which she tied back or wore in braids. She had wanted to cut her hair short once, but Son had persuaded her not to, and to please him she had left it long. Her body was muscular in a feminine way and lithe, like that of a young deer.

But it was Shaw's face that was really striking. Her features were sharp and clear-cut, with an expression in the eyes and around the mouth that shouted out vitality and joy of living. Her eyes were rather almond-shaped, although large, and her cheekbones were somewhat prominent. But whatever jaggedness might have been in that face was smoothed over, softened, by her expressive personality.

Shaw was self-confident without being aggressive. She was self-contained without being withdrawn. She knew she could do anything any boy her own age could do, and usually do it better, and besides which she was bright and able to do her schoolwork to her own satisfaction at least.

Anyway, that's the way it was out in the country, where houses were far between and where daughters were encouraged to be strong.

Shaw was angry. Son could see that.

"Why are you spending so much time with that Adams girl? What's her name? Cindy? You never used to like her. Since you got that pick-up you've been taking her home and leaving me to ride the bus alone. Are you my friend or not? I thought we were blood-friends. . . . Son, what's wrong? Don't you want to do things with me anymore?"

She looked as if she might cry but Son knew she wouldn't. She never did.

"Shaw, you and I talked about this once before. You remember when Mr. Jones put our cow in with his bull? You remember then we talked about men and women and what they did."

"Are you doing that with Cindy Adams?" she almost screamed.

"No, no. But it's like I told you then. When a boy grows up, he starts to liking girls in a different way. He starts thinking different. He doesn't just want to run around and play. I love you, Shaw, but you're like a sister. And you're almost two years younger than me. Things have got to change some. I've got to have other friends now. I don't know exactly what's happening. But I like to be with Cindy, too. She's different from you. I don't feel the same about her as I do about you. You're still my special friend, my buddy."

Shaw got up and stood there like a statue for a few moments. Then she turned and walked slowly away, running after a few seconds. For the first time in years she cried, but Son could not see.

He called after her, but she was gone.

After Son graduated from high school, he went off to Haskell Indian Junior College. His departure enlarged the empty place in Shaw's life. During the previous year she had still been able to spend some time with him, and there had been moments when she had almost forgotten the changes taking place.

But after he left she realized that she was truly alone and that her feeling of sadness was not apt to go away.

Shaw had started going out with boys. It was easy at first, because she was used to associating with Son and his friends, but she found that the boys were gradually leaving her alone, not asking her to dances or taking her home after school.

One guy, Bob, did take her to a dance, though. He kept going outside to drink and afterward, in the car, he grabbed Shaw and started kissing her.

She closed her eyes and tried to enjoy it, but his liquor breath and rough lips repelled her. Still, she put up with it because it seemed to her that that's what boys wanted.

After a little while he began breathing more heavily, and she felt an insistent hand grasp hold of one of her breasts. Shaw tried to push him away, but he kept rubbing and squeezing, using his other hand to reach up her dress, touching her thigh.

Shaw knew that the boy was all worked up like a stallion but she didn't feel like a mare in heat. What he was doing just seemed like an invasion of her private self, the using of a body that was hers, not his. So she pushed him away with all her might and raised a fist to hit him, shouting at the same time, "Bob, you're drunk. I don't want you feeling me all over. You try it again and I'm goin' to slug you. . . . You better take me home."

"Oh, shit, goddamn it, Shaw, you are just a P-T, a goddamn fuckin' P-T. When are you goin' to wise up? If you want a guy to take you out, you've got to do somethin' nice for him. What do you think everybody else is doin' now?"

"You mean all of the other girls let you guys do what you want to? I don't believe that."

"Shaw, goddamn it. Oh, my balls ache! Listen, some girls don't go out at all, because they don't do nothin', that's why. Others only go out with pip-squeaks who are afraid to try anything. If you want to be popular, you've got to make out!"

Shaw just glared at him. Finally she said, "Bob, take me home. I'll have to think it over. I just don't feel like anything more tonight."

Bob started to turn on the engine, but then he turned to her, pleading, "Please, Shaw, I'm in pain. You don't know how it is. You don't have to do nothin'. Just rub me, please. I got to have some relief."

Shaw didn't want to do anything, but inside she was desperate to be accepted. She said, "Okay."

Bob moved close and opened up his pants, sliding them and his shorts down to his knees. Shaw was surprised at how big his organ was, but she did as he asked and touched it. He kissed her and fondled her some while she rubbed, slowly at first and then harder as he became more excited.

After he was all done he drove her home and said he'd like to take her out again. She ran into the house without answering.

Shaw spent a great deal of time by herself, thinking about Bob and the other boys. She thought about Son, too, but quickly erased him from her mind whenever he appeared.

The truth was that she didn't like making out with

boys. On the other hand, she *was* lonely and she *did* want to learn to do what girls were supposed to do.

The next time Shaw got a chance to go out she drank liquor with the boys and, afterward, in the back seat of an old car, she let one of them go all the way. She was dry, he was inept, and the whole thing was very painful and disappointing.

Still, he seemed elated and Shaw felt that maybe it would get better, now that she was no longer a virgin. It didn't, though.

Try as she might she just couldn't get excited. The huffing and puffing of the boy only made her feel more alone, more left out. She tried to pretend, but only the boys were fooled, ecstatic in their ignorance and egotism.

In fact, Shaw began to picture the male sex organ as a sort of enemy designed only to hurt her. She had always wished that she were a boy like Son, and now she began to resent her fate very much.

Still, she tried and tried.

Shaw never did graduate from that high school. About the middle of the year she was expelled, and her parents in great haste sent her off to a Bureau of Indian Affairs boarding school. She finally graduated after being transferred to a different, tougher school, but she never went back home.

Son was away about four years, intermittently going to college and working. After Shaw's letters stopped coming, he just let the days and months go by without trying to find out what had happened. When he got home he noticed right away that something was wrong. Nobody would say anything about her, except that she had left, probably for good. Son sensed that something very serious had happened, but all that his folks would say was, "No use talkin' about it. What's done is done. It can't be changed now."

Son tried to relax in his old environment. He had half-planned to take up stock raising and use his savings to improve the old place. Still, nothing seemed the same. Most of his friends were gone and without Shaw the place seemed empty.

He wandered around for a few weeks, trying to get a better feeling. Following old trails, fishing the creeks, riding along familiar ridges, all of these things just brought back memories of Shaw.

It came to him then that he really loved her with a terrible longing. She had grown to be a part of him, a part he had tried to ignore but just couldn't suppress any longer. To himself he said, "I tried to think of her as a sister. Thinking that way I ignored her figure, her pretty legs, her eyes, her smile—I just buried them. But all the time they were there anyway. I was just kidding myself."

Son then set out, single-mindedly, to dig up every clue he could as to her whereabouts. But nobody knew, not even her parents. No one had gotten so much as a postcard from her.

So he set out in his car, driving to the last boarding school she had attended, even though it was many hundreds of miles away. Even that journey seemed a waste of time, however, until he ran into a teacher who remembered her. The teacher offered one clue: "She was really close to one girl, a Shoshone from Fort Hall, Nellie Fitch. I think they left together, to go to the big city together. They were really good friends. If you can find Nellie, she will know where Shaw is."

Son was able to get Nellie's home address and parents' names. With that he drove to Fort Hall, not knowing anything else to do. Nellie's parents knew nothing about Shaw, but they said that Nellie had gone to San

Francisco on relocation. They hadn't heard from her in many months, but they assumed she was still there.

So it was off to San Francisco for Son. He was beginning to get a little tired and his money was running low, but he figured that he could get a job or enroll in college in California and continue looking for Shaw.

In San Francisco and Oakland he visited all of the Indian centers and bars looking for Shaw or Nellie. He finally found Nellie working in a laundry. Her response was an angry one when he asked about Shaw: "I don't know where she is and I don't give a damn either. We haven't been friends for a long time."

"But what was she doing when you last saw her?"

"She was working as a cocktail waitress in a bar up around North Beach. But she left there, I think. We were living together but she moved out. I don't know where she went."

With very few clues, Son took a break from his search, getting a part-time job and enrolling at San Francisco State College. Finally, he put ads in local papers and talked to people at neighborhood centers. In one of them he picked up the idea of checking with the Department of Motor Vehicles to see if she had a driver's license. She didn't.

But Son kept looking.

It was a second-class bar with a jazz band featured at night.

Shaw recognized Son as soon as he walked in, even though his hair was long and his face was older. Her first reaction was to run toward him; her second was to run away.

She did neither. Instead she watched his face.

He was looking around but the dimness of the bar delayed his reaction. Finally, seeing Shaw, his face turned all smiles and with unmistakable joy he rushed over to her, hugging her tightly.

"Shaw, I've been looking for you for months, all over the place, everywhere. At last I've found you!"

"Son!" was all she could say. But then, noticing the stares of patrons, she guided him to a table and added, "Sit down, please. I'll get you a drink. What do you want?"

"Nothing really. You're enough. I've been drinking in every bar in San Francisco looking for you. But I'll have a beer to keep the bartender happy. Shaw! It's so good to see you. I've got so much to tell you."

"I've got a lot to tell you, too, Son. And I'm glad to see you, really glad. . . . I'll get your beer."

The place was not very busy, so Shaw asked the other waitress to take over for her for a while. Then she joined Son at the table, nervously lighting up a cigarette, trying to get time to think. "How much does he know?" she thought to herself.

Son reached out and took her hand, squeezing it hard. Then he put his arm around her, still squeezing her hand, not saying a word, with tears forming in his eyes.

"You're hurting my hand," she said with a smile, her own eyes becoming moist.

"I'm sorry. Oh, Shaw, how much I've missed you. My life has been tied up around the memory of you for these past months. Now I've got to touch you to know you're real, in the flesh, at last!"

"I may not be the same as your memories, Son. I hope you're not disappointed that you found me . . . someday."

"I won't be. Shaw, I know you had some trouble. I don't care what it was. You mean too much to me. . . ."

"Tell me, Son, how did you find me?" She tried to change the subject, hoping as well to see what he knew.

He told her everything that had happened, going back to when he had left home to go to Haskell. When he was finished he added, "I love you, Shaw. I want to see you when you get off work so I can talk with you more."

She sat there for awhile, with a half-smile flickering on her face, covering up the terrible knot of fear in her stomach. He didn't really know anything. And when he found out? It was better not to see him again, she thought, and yet she wanted to be with him.

She looked over at him, touching his arm gently. "It makes me feel so good to see you, Son. I have to go back to work now, but I can get off early. . . . Why don't you meet me somewhere and we can have a late dinner?"

They agreed upon a place. Son kissed her on the cheek and left in a dream of joy. Outside he jumped up and down a couple of times and ran off as if he were a kid, frightening a number of pedestrians who chanced to see him.

The week went by very happily for Son. He and Shaw got together as much as possible. They talked endlessly about their common memories and spent a lot of time walking together in Golden Gate Park, at the zoo, along the marina, and at Fisherman's Wharf. They rode cable cars everywhere, watched Chinese people buying smoked ducks and fish in Chinatown, and ate dinner in a little family-operated café nearby.

For Son it was an intensely romantic time. He was obviously very much in love. Still, he never did more than kiss Shaw on the cheek, hold her hands, or hug her. The truth was that he was shy somehow. Maybe he sensed a reluctance, a hesitancy in her. More likely he just couldn't quite break the habit of the many years of treating her like a sister.

Shaw enjoyed being with him very much. At times she pretended that they were back in the country and were children again. She was relieved that he didn't try to make love to her, but she enjoyed his touch.

When they were separate, though, when she was all alone, the bitter truth rose up like vomit into her throat and fear made her shake. She dreaded each new day and yet she couldn't stay away. She didn't know how to tell Son the truth. She didn't want to hurt him or drive him away. "But it will happen. Sooner or later, it will happen. I'll have to hurt him. I'm so afraid of his love. I can feel his love growing day by day, but it scares me. It's a different kind of love now. He sees me as a woman. Not a sister anymore. A woman. Maybe I can tell him I'm in love with somebody else. That will hurt, but not as much as the truth will."

One day Son drove her to Muir Woods, and after wandering beneath the redwoods, they drove to the top of a high ridge, watching the fog creeping up on the hills from the west.

Son kissed her on the lips for a long time. It didn't feel bad to Shaw. In fact, it felt good, because he was gentle and his lips were soft on hers, but still she was petrified, immobile.

He started caressing her, telling her how he loved her more than anyone in the world and wanted to be with her always. "This is it," she said to herself. "The crisis. What should I do?" Thoughts of committing suicide came to her mind. She could just jump in front of a car and he might believe it was an accident.

Then she thought, "Maybe I can let him love me. It will give him pleasure, and I'll get pleasure knowing that he's enjoying it. . . . No, it wouldn't last. I couldn't fool Son, not forever."

She gently broke loose from his embrace and said out loud, "Son, I'm a little tired and hungry from all this fog and cold air. Why don't we go to dinner? And then maybe we can dance afterward."

Her ruse worked and they found a quiet place to eat and then to dance. But Shaw was tense and she drank her cocktails rapidly, having one after another. "I'm getting drunk on purpose, just like the first time I got laid," she said to herself. "Poor Son, poor me," she added.

While driving back to the city Shaw got up her courage. She said, "Son, I do love you. I've always loved you. Because of that I have to tell you everything. We can't go on like this with you not knowing what I'm really like. It's going to hurt—me as well as you. Do you want to hear?"

He said yes in a half-inaudible, throaty voice.

She went on. She told him all about her loneliness, her escapades with boys, her efforts at sex and how she had failed, both at home and since. She told him how she had learned to fool men.

"It's easy, although I don't like it. Most of them are so hung up on themselves they're not paying any attention to the woman anyway. Some of them just don't care. As long as you wiggle a little and groan here and there, they're fooled. Some don't even worry about that. As long as they've shot their wad, they just assume everything's okay, like it's a privilege to just be lying with them, like that's enough for any woman."

Liquor loosened her tongue and she said more than she had intended. Son was silent for a long time, but finally he interrupted:

"Shaw, it's all right. I've had sex with other girls. I hope I've been a better lover than the guys you describe, but anyway, I'm no virgin and I didn't expect you to be. I don't care about all that. I love you, don't you see? I know that I can make you feel good, because I really care about you. Maybe it will take time, but I got plenty of time. Bad experiences have only made you think you're frigid. We can be patient with each other and work it out."

He reached out to touch her, but she shrank away.

"Son, I haven't finished yet. It's not just that I don't enjoy sex with men. There's more."

She paused and he was silent.

"Son, I've discovered that I like other women. That's why I got kicked out of school and had to leave. That's why I can't go back home. That's why I have no family. That's why I can't have you."

For several days Son wandered around by himself, mostly along the beach. All of his dreams were shattered. He was tortured by images of Shaw in bed with other women. He was jealous and hurt, feeling very sorry for himself.

Gradually, however, he began to feel more sorry for Shaw. And he realized that love was something he couldn't just cast aside, like a bottle that had been drained.

"She did say she loved me. So she does! She still loves me, and I still love her. I don't care if she has slept with women. That's no worse than having sex with men. Maybe it isn't even as serious. If I truly love her, I should try to help her."

So he met her after work. Shaw was surprised to see him, pleased in fact, because she had given him up for good and had suffered just as he had.

They had dinner, a silent dinner, and then drove out by the marina where they could watch boats bob up and down and see the lights across the Golden Gate in Marin County.

"Shaw, I still love you. Just as much as ever. I want to help you. I want you to marry me or, at least, live with me. I know that, little by little, we can pull it off."

"And what if we can't? What if I want to slip out to go with another woman? What then? I love you, Son, but not in a physical way. No, that's wrong. I do love you physically but not sexually. Can you understand? I love to have you hug me. I love your body as part of you, my friend Son. You *are* handsome to me, and I like to have you close . . . but I don't feel anything sexy. I just don't."

"But Shaw, maybe you will change. Gradually. I'll be real tender and gentle. It will all work out."

"You have to accept me for what I am, Son. Anything else would be a lie. I would only hurt you more. I don't want to do that."

He was silent for a long time, staring off toward Alcatraz. Then he blurted out, "It's not natural! You've got to try to change. Shaw, you've got to."

"Take me home, Son, or I'll walk if you want me to. I have tried to change and I can't."

He drove her silently to her apartment house and she got out without a word being exchanged. Finally, in parting, she said, "You've been a good friend, Son, my best friend. Don't worry about me. Don't even think about me. Find someone else."

She ran up the stairs.

He sat there in his car for a long while staring at nothing.

For several weeks Shaw didn't see Son at all. The ache in her heart remained constant, and she had no thoughts in which he didn't intrude. His friendship meant so much to her.

She kept busy, though, taking classes at City College and working at night. Shaw was resourceful and although she suffered a great deal, somehow she was strong enough to go on with life. She had plans for herself and although they seemed less important now, she hoped that with time her enthusiasm could come back.

Son, on the other hand, was too miserable to continue with his job and classes. He needed to get away, to try to break the train of thought he was locked into, always torturing himself with thoughts of Shaw.

He heard about an Indian spiritual conference out in the country and, on the spur of the moment, he decided to go there. When he got a chance he sought out a medicine man who had impressed him with the depth of his wisdom. Son told him all about Shaw. The medicine man looked hard at Son.

"There are two things that I can say. The first is this: the Creator has made every creature different. Not even two birds of the same kind are exactly alike. Each one of us is unique. We are all the same and yet different. The Creator seems to like it that way. Each person has their own personal gifts and individual dreams. Those things cannot be changed. We have to respect them so long as they don't harm others. We have to respect each other. At the same time it is also possible that some great wrong might cause a person to go against their real dreams, their real gifts. But no one else can change that. We can only help. But each person has to find their own way. We cannot invent dreams for another creature. It is foolish to try."

Then he paused, watching Son closely.

"The second thing is this: you must look closely into your own heart. Do you love this person, or do you love yourself? Of course, you must love yourself before you can truly love another, but what I mean is different. It is this: do you need to *possess* her to love her? Do you have to own her? Is she supposed to do something for you? Is your love a downpayment on something you expect to get in return? Now only you can look into your heart and see what is there. Love between a man and a woman is a wonderful thing and, in marriage, it has to go both ways to be truly good, to last a lifetime.

"But there are many other kinds of love, all beautiful, like the love of a parent for a child, of a sister for a brother, or of a friend for a friend. What kind of love are you seeking? You must ask yourself.

"That's all I can say to you, except this: in the old days our peoples had women who dreamed men's dreams and who lived as men. I guess there were not many of them, but there were some, not in every tribe but in quite a few. Now these women were allowed to grow up as men. What else could we have done? You cannot change a person's inner spirit by force! That only creates a monster or kills them, destroys them. So we had such people. Sometimes they were only tolerated. Sometimes they were respected. But we did not try to change them."

Son went off by himself after the gathering, fishing along mountain streams and sitting still in quiet places. His torture had ended, because his mind had stopped grinding itself to pieces. Instead he felt rather dull, as if he was half-asleep or doped.

But gradually, in that quiet state, he made up his mind, decided what he wanted to do.

Shaw was just coming out of one of her classes at college when she saw Son. He waved to her and she panicked inside. She was just beginning to feel somewhat normal again and now here he was to create a new surge of turmoil.

Son came up before she could turn away. He could see the frightened look in her face and he chose his words carefully: "Shaw, I'm not here to hurt you anymore. Don't be afraid of me. Don't turn away. Will you give me a chance to talk to you?"

"All right," she said.

They found a quiet place and sat down on the grass. He said, "I've missed you. I always do. I'm sorry about what I said the other night, but can you blame a person who's in love? Can you blame me? I've got a right to go off the deep end at times. . . . So do you. Anyway, I've been doing a lot of thinking and feeling. Shaw, I want to be your friend, your true friend, forever. I love you. Do you understand?"

"I don't know, Son. I want to be your friend . . . but do you really think that a man and a woman can be true friends? I mean without sex, or at least without the potential of sex? Or do you just want what you wanted the other night—conditional friendship with the secret hope of sex someday?"

"That's what I thought of, too, Shaw. That's the question I asked. But first let me tell you something else. I thought to myself: if I love Shaw, then I have to love *her* as she is, not some myth or some dream of her. And I have to give her my love as a gift with no strings attached."

"I have to respect you, Shaw. After all, how can I love you if I don't respect you? I mean, I might not respect your drinking if you drank too much, but you, as a person, with your own path to follow, I have to respect that. I guess it's hard to *really* love someone. Because it means setting them free."

He took her hand and hugged her. She was stiff at first, but soon she hugged him in return, although with a degree of tentativeness.

"I want you to be free, Shaw. I don't want to own you. I'll help whenever you need help, and I hope you'll want to help me, but I'll only intrude when invited."

"But can it really be done, Son? I don't see it happening much. You'll have to find another woman to satisfy your other needs. I don't know. She'll be jealous of me if she knows about us."

"I'll cross that bridge when I come to it, Shaw. Listen, what I came to realize was that I always used to love you as a sister. I still love you that way, and more. I can't promise you that I won't think of you sexually, because you're so beautiful to me, but I think I can keep that under control. The main thing is: it has to be possible for men and women to be friends, to love each other, without going to bed."

He took her hand again and asked, "Will you be my friend? Knowing that I'm only human and may make mistakes and do stupid things, will you still be my friend?"

Tears were in his eyes and Shaw, feeling a sense of happiness she hadn't felt for more than four years, let her own tears flow freely. She hugged him hard, holding him tight up against her, squeezing *his* hand.

"Son, ever since I was old enough to walk and talk I've been loving you. You're my family, Son. My friend!"

"I'm glad to be home!"

SOMEONE TO LOVE

"PLEASE SEND ME SOMEONE TO LOVE" WAS MY PRAYER. My heart sent its melody through my being every minute. And at night I dreamed of the loved one.

And yet there was no one.

"I'm just a lonely boy. . . . I been thinkin about drinkin'. . . . Won't someone please help me lose these lonesome boy blues?. . . Oh, man . . ."

And I was drinking. Liquor helped me create a false sense of being at ease, and then it helped me suffer, descend into the depths of self-pity and solitude.

Sometimes I drank to fool other people. The white girls, the ones who didn't seem to find my Indian looks so attractive, well, at least they could see my swagger and smell the wine on my breath. I was tough, they thought. Rough.

It was all a lie, but I would rather have died than let them know how soft, how sensitive, how lonely I really was. Not lonely for company—I had friends. But these friends were like me, all hungering after something we could never give each other.

The truth is, I worshiped girls. I needed some woman's love so badly that I could feel the lack as a physical part of me.

One night I went to a party. An Italian guy, a casual friend, had a little pad and he sent the word out through all of his connections. So I went.

There were a lot of people at the party and I started drinking and dancing. I don't know exactly when, but at some point I became aware that a Mexican woman was there whom I had never seen before. She was brown and pretty and I started watching her. Soon I asked her to dance.

It was like magic. I had never thought of myself as a good dancer, but on that night, with her, I felt smooth and sure. After one dance I had no desire for anyone else, and neither had she. From then on we danced differently from anything I had known before. Her body became part of mine and mine part of hers.

Hours went by as we held each other close. The way she pressed against me told me that she liked me as no woman ever had before.

I felt very good and yet, out of habit or maybe out of an underlying fear, I kept on drinking. In between the dances I drank a little—not too much but it all added up.

Still, she didn't seem to mind. I brushed my hand in her hair and kissed her a little while we were pressed close together. All of the repressed desires, hopes, and needs of many years channeled themselves into my touches. She held me tightly, too, and I knew she needed the love as much as I.

Late in the evening, or early in the morning, I didn't have any idea of the time, we went outside to my car. The cool air hit me and I was really drunk, drunk with wine, drunk with passion.

At first everything was wonderful. I kissed her lips, her cheeks, her ears, her nose, and then her lips again. Passion overwhelmed me, utterly seized control, and soon I was touching her breasts and then my hand moved to her leg. Of its own will my hand moved lovingly but insistently along her thigh.

She stopped me and said, "Wait, I have to go to the bathroom. I'll be back in just a minute."

I let her crawl out of the car. I was so drunk, but still in an expectant mood, I waited.

How long I was out there I'll never know. I started getting cold, but I was so drunk that the world just floated around me in a haze.

At last I became uneasy and went looking for her.

She was nowhere to be found. Her girlfriend was gone, too. No one knew anything about them.

It took me a long time to realize what had happened. She was gone and I had been too drunk to even get her address. I didn't so much as know her last name or what part of the city she lived in.

She was gone and I was still praying for someone to love.

A CITY INDIAN GOES TO SCHOOL

THEY MANAGED TO PICK UP SEVERAL PINTS OF WHISKEY but made the mistake of not drinking it right away. Hunger overtook them, so they stopped in a little café to eat. It was already late and the place was almost empty, so they started playing blackjack and poker. The owner didn't bother them. They kept on playing, hand after hand, nobody winning too much, just passing the money back and forth. Engrossed with gambling, the boys ate sandwiches and drank lots of coffee. They just kept on, long after the food had been finished.

Eventually the owner wanted to close for the night. The boys went out and piled into Carlos Villagutierre's twenty-year-old, 1934 Ford sedan. They started out, continuing along the mountain road toward the place where they planned to camp out. They had stayed too long. All the gas stations, and there weren't many of them anyway, were closed and Carlos's gas gauge was nearly empty. Luckily they could coast for a while. Jim Many Geese knew the route, so he told Carlos to just coast off the ridge and down toward Big Bear Valley. They saved what gas was left, but coasting slowed them down.

Finally they got to Big Bear Lake. Almost everything was closed but they managed to get some gas. They went on to an area that Jim knew about, where no people lived, out in the trees.

"Hey, Jim, it's dark out here! No lights at all."

"And, man, it is cold!"

"Well, we still have that rotgut, so let's warm up the inside first. Gimme one of those bottles."

"Damn, we should have got something to mix it with. This stuff is strong!"

"It does taste kind of corky, too—funny tasting."

"Cheap whiskey, man, that's what it is."

"Aw, cut out the talk. Let a man drink. I'll show you how it's done."

"Shit, man, that stuff really hits hard. No food in the stomach to soften that stuff down. Wow! I feel high already."

"Where are the girls, Jim? Behind that tree? Let's go look for them. Girls, girls, where are you? Come out and meet your lover!"

Soon they got warmed up. Silly, crazy even, they started jumping around on logs, yelling, running all over, kidding each other, just drunk out in nowhere. They killed all of the bottles. What a waste! Not of the whiskey. It was no good anyway. Just a waste of energy, for no purpose, just to get high out in the cold, in the dark, no campfire even.

Shivering when they slowed down, the boys gradually became depressed. The liquor changed its chemicals in their bloodstreams. Low-spirited now, and cold, they gradually gave up and crawled into their sleeping bags or blankets. Drunk, they went to sleep very late.

Long after the sun had risen high in the sky Jim awakened. The bright light blinded him. His throat was dry and sour, bitter tasting. His head ached, his stomach felt hungry but uneasy, too. When he stood up he was dizzy and his head throbbed. Weakly he walked over to a bush and pissed. His stomach sent up a spray of bitter gall, but he swallowed it back down. Jim felt like puking but he held the vomit down. "I need some 7 Up or something to help my stomach," he thought.

One by one the other guys managed to get up. Several looked pale. They all felt hot in the sun, a funny kind of feverish heat. Their movements were haphazard, weak, lacking in motivation, groping; they were moving in pain, with great effort. But they couldn't stay there. They were all hungry for something, something to ease their pain, to make their mouths taste good again.

Carlos drove them to a café–grocery store several miles away. Most of them were too sick to go in. They just sat on the road by the car and ached, begging for something. Jim started to go in, but the smell of food turned his stomach and he stopped. He couldn't go in. One of the guys brought out some 7 Up. They tried to drink it but couldn't. Just a little bit, then they had to stop. Larry Redwing started throwing up.

Jim tried to smoke a cigarette. It tasted awful.

Several guys were puking now.

Jim threw up.

They couldn't stay there. People were looking at them. The cops might come. They couldn't stay anywhere. They couldn't go anywhere. Nothing was possible. Groping, they were too sick to cope. Rotgut whiskey was still in them, eating at their insides.

Finally Carlos started the car and they got in. For miles they drove aimlessly, Larry leaning out the door, puking, holding on to the door handle, almost falling out. At first Carlos stopped, but then he just kept going. Others puked but not so often.

Jim managed to smoke, got control of his stomach but still couldn't eat. They kept on driving. Larry was still throwing up, only yellow green bile now, no food left. They were worried about him. At first it was kind of funny, but he was really sick. Later he was just puking nothing; just air was coming up and still he couldn't stop.

Hours went by. They got to a little lake with a store and Jim managed to start eating milk and soda crackers, lots of crackers. He started out carefully and finally got it down. Gradually he began to feel better. Everybody was able to get something down now, except Larry.

When they got back to L.A. that night, Larry was still sick, but he had finally stopped heaving. He got out and went into his house without a word. He couldn't talk.

Jim never saw Larry drink again. It would have been good if Jim had learned the same lesson, but all he could figure out was that the whiskey was poison and that the clever thing to do was to drink tequila or vodka—alcohol without contamination in it.

Jim started cutting school a lot at about that time, especially around the tenth grade. It wasn't just that he disliked the classes. It was more that he loved freedom. He loved to be outdoors, walking freely in the fresh air and sunshine, or sitting in a coffee shop smoking a cigarette, or roaming the used bookstores, record shops, and streets of downtown L.A., or hitchhiking to the beach or to the mountains.

There was something exquisite, strangely exhilarating, about being on one's own during midday hours when others were still locked up in poorly lit buildings, reading nonsense, their minds wandering because of the dullness of it all.

Of course, lots of people cut classes. Sometimes Jim had friends along. But Jim and his friends were a little different from most kids, who just wasted their time drinking or smoking reefers. Jim had little use for *marijuanos* and although he drank, he had no desire to be a wino. He knew too well, from what he heard from his Mexicano friends, about *los marijuanos* and how they just kind of groped around in a fog all day long, stumbling around in the barrio. And Jim saw plenty of winos on East Fifth Street and Main Street. Their stench and aimless lives, hanging around dairy-lunch places until being kicked out and then vomiting out front to get revenge on the shopkeepers, and the scary look of the dives they went into, and the drab flophouses some of them lived in, all of these things Jim learned about in his "school without walls."

The Follies burlesque house, many little record stores, and some used bookshops were crowded in along Main between B-girl bars and clip joints of all kinds. Main Street was pretty seedy, but Jim looked older than his age and he even went into the burlesque theater once with a couple of buddies. It was a one-time experience, because the place stank and the men in there were somewhat odd. The dancers looked sexy and all, but if you looked hard you could see that most of them were already old and wrinkled and heavily powdered. It wasn't much, the friends decided.

Every once in awhile he would run into an Indian wino down there. This always shook him up, because the guy would sometimes recognize Jim as an Indian and come up close, asking for money. Jim could smell the layers upon layers of muscatel or tokay and it kind of scared him, it was so strong—and the men's faces and eyes! The face was usually all bright red, the redness oozing up through the brown skin, especially around the puffed up, swollen nose, and lots of times the skin was full of little holes or boils or pimples. The eyes were blurry, somewhat vacant, but also sometimes sad, sometimes scary.

Jim didn't understand the Indian winos. He felt sorry for them and afraid of them. He thought that he could drink a little and still never be like them. He didn't really see the connection between getting drunk and being a wino. Only later did he come to understand things better.

The school newspaper helped Jim a lot. Because of his interest in drawing, he decided to sign up for journalism class. It was a good class, because he and some of the other guys got to take a car and go off campus to the printing plant where the paper was published. This gave them a chance to smoke and drink coffee without cutting classes. Jim also got to go to other high schools to cover sports events and put a lot of his drawings in the paper. In fact, it was his work as an illustrator that secured him a place on the staff.

The other students were pleased with Jim's drawings, even though he had to sneak many of them in at the last minute. "Hey, those drawings are good, Jimmy-boy; they look like us," said Carlos. And indeed the drawings were of athletes, cheerleaders, and students in general who had Indian or African or Asian racial features. The principal tried to stop Jim, using the journalism teacher as his mouthpiece:

"Jimmy, why don't you just draw *ordinary* people? Why do you want to draw attention to racial differences? Let's not single anyone out. We want to treat everyone the same—all equal. Some students may feel bad if attention is drawn to the ways they are different."

Because he was a good illustrator, Jim was able to get away with innovations in art—but not so with his writing. He got called into the principal's office one day for writing an article on "Warren G. Harding: Our First Nonwhite President."

The principal said, "You're a good writer, James, and you've done a lot of work on this piece, but I can't allow it to be printed."

"But it's the truth," responded Jim. "I checked out

a couple of books and Harding's family was classed as colored."

"But it's too shocking, James. What will people think? People from downtown look over our paper. Parents read our paper. And students might be influenced by it."

"I don't get it! What's so bad about Harding being part colored!"

"James, people like to look up to the presidency. We like to think of the president as being the highest type of person. We don't want to tear that image down. We have to teach good citizenship here. That's the basic source of all of our democratic values."

"But are you saying that I have no right to be the president someday just because I'm Indian?"

"No, James, I'm not saying that. But you know that your chances of being president are nonexistent, not because of what I say but because of—well, because— because it takes many, many generations to develop a high civilization, and well, people don't just acquire that stature in a few years."

Jim started to turn away in disgust, but the principal got in a parting shot: "The big danger, James, is that your article might suggest to some of our more impressionable young people, and to our parents as well, that we *approve* of interracial dating and marriage—whites with nonwhites. I mean, after all, if President Harding was really of mixed race, a colored man with a white wife . . ."

But Jim didn't hear the rest.

And the same thing happened later with an article he wrote on the Indian village of Ya, buried by then under the railroad station downtown. He made the mistake of telling how the Indians were still being sold as slaves in the city plaza as late as 1869 and how the first Spanish-speaking settlers of Los Angeles were all of Indian or African blood.

The principal called him in again. "James, you can't present one-sided ideas that will generate resentment and race hate. Here you are telling how the Indians were sold as slaves, but you don't balance that with all of the good things the Americans did for them—such as schools and Christianity and democracy."

"I could talk about that. Indians were kept out of the white schools for years, and they were already Catholics when the Anglo-Saxons came here."

"Who is it you are calling Anglo-Saxons?" asked the principal. "Do you mean the Americans?"

Jim kind of gritted his teeth and responded, "I don't know what else to call them since the Indians were already Americans—the real Americans—before the *gavachos* got here, and the Mexicans were already Americans, too. I mean Mexico is a part of North America. I believe I learned that in geography."

The conversation almost went no further. The principal said, "That's the end of this. You will write no more articles. Don't ever call the American people by some dirty Spanish name like that. You are a troublemaker, boy. You are headed for a lot of trouble for yourself, too, unless you learn to appreciate our democracy. Preaching race hate! Being a rebel! That will get you nowhere. I can assure you of that."

"But, sir," said Jim, "the textbooks this school uses are always preaching hate toward Indians. They're full of lies. Here, I have a list of things they say that are insulting to me and my family, like these. I'll read some."

"A handful of savages could not and should not have remained unaltered at the expense of a higher form of life."

"The story of the United States is that of a series of frontiers that the hand of man has reclaimed from nature and the savage."

"The Indian is a savage, noxious animal, and his actions are those of a ferocious beast of prey."

"But this great land, when the Europeans first entered it, was only an untamed wilderness thinly occupied by tribes of Indians. It had to be possessed and transformed."

"It is well to remember that American society is definitely European in origin."

"The story of the American people is fairly short if it be dated from . . . Jamestown in 1607. . . . But, of course, the American Story actually begins in Europe."

The principal looked perplexed and said, "James, these are not attacks made by illiterate racists in Mississippi or in some cowboy bar in South Dakota. No, they are very carefully thought out assertions made by America's most eminent historians writing in the standard texts or reference works used in high schools and colleges all over this land of ours. Many of these historians have won prizes!"

"Prizes from whom?" shouted Jim. "Not from Indians, or Mexicans, or Negroes! Those writers have probably killed a lot of my people with their words. . . . They've at least done a lot of damage. And, I guess, just like you say, they do it consciously, on purpose, with guns blazing for white supremacy. I guess they're your war heroes, just like Custer and that general who said, 'The only good Indians I ever saw were dead.' I guess your historians are soldiers, soldiers fighting to destroy our minds."

"They're just *gavachos* to me!" And with that Jim stormed out of the office, feeling terribly angry but also somehow elated. He now knew about that principal and why the school was so bad.

Years later he was able to easily understand the Bureau of Indian Affairs and its psychology after going through the L.A. public schools, strange as this may seem.

The school library was no good. They were careful not to have anything improper there. The local branch library had a few things, but not much on Indians. It was the downtown public library, safely insulated by distance from most children, that held the key. How did Jim find it?

Not too far from Jim's house, in a somewhat hilly area littered with old oil wells, lived a man who was a friend of Jim's father. Jim used to go there to listen to the two of them talk. Américo López was a truly exceptional, self-educated man and his house was full of old *National Geographics*, *Americas*, and other magazines with articles about Indians, ancient American civilizations, and other nonwhite peoples and places. López also had many books, usually purchased used and worn out by then but still readable. This was Jim's first real library.

He would sit for hours half-listening to the men's talk while poring through old magazines. Then he borrowed books, especially ones about Indians, or Mexico, or wild animals and strange lands. Here it was that he discovered A. Hyatt Verrill's *Our Indians* and *Ancient Civilizations of the New World* and, more important, books by Black Elk, Plenty Coups, Luther Standing Bear, and others.

Black Elk Speaks became an inspiration to Jim. For years he couldn't understand its meaning in depth, but many passages hit him like the breath of an eagle feather, cleansing him of evil, and making his mind sane and strong.

Black Elk started out: "What is one man that he should make much of his winters, even when they bend him like a heavy snow? So many other men have lived and shall live that story, to be grass upon the hills." Something hit Jim very hard. Black Elk sounded like the old Indians of his grandparents' generation. His words sounded like the breeze of leaves in the trees. They poured forth gently but with the immense power of flowing water.

"It is the story of all life that is holy and is good to tell, and of us two-leggeds sharing in it with the four-leggeds and the wings of the air and all green things, for these are children of one mother and their father is one Spirit."

He was pulled into the story and could not leave, not for eating or for sleeping.

"Great Spirit, Great Spirit, my Grandfather, all over the earth the faces of living things are all alike. With tenderness have these come up out of the ground. Look upon these faces of children without number and with children in their arms, that they may face the winds and walk the good road to the day of quiet."

Jim, like millions of other young people, and millions of older ones, too, was facing the hard winds of a racist society and of an imperialistic age in which he was only a number, a living machine to be drafted and sent off to kill or be killed, a living paper-shuffler to be cooped up in an office for forty years or more, or a living shovel to move dirt for somebody else. He didn't realize all of that yet, but he did sense that Black Elk's words were like a bright beam of sunshine piercing through dark clouds.

He now knew, beyond any shadow of doubt, that the teachers lied, that the textbooks lied, that the movies lied, that he was surrounded by lies. Because here, right in his hands was a book with the words of an Indian who spoke with a quality of spirituality, compassion, genius, and wisdom that he had never found before in any source. And he was an Indian! A savage! A heathen!

By what miracle had such a book been allowed to exist? Were there others? Jim went on searching and he found many things, including an anthology of Indian prose and poetry. In it, under Delaware, he read, "Truly we are thankful that we have lived long enough to see the time come when these our grandfathers the trees bloom forth, and also the coming up of vegetation.

"Now as well for this water and for him our grandfather fire, and again the air, again this sunlight. When everyone has been blessed with such gifts it is enough to make one realize what kind of benevolence come from our fathers, because he it is who has created everything."

Jim knew only a little about the old Big House ceremonies, but now he was reading the speeches given at one forty years before.

"It is said traditionally, when anyone on Good meditates in his heart, there is formed the thought. And when he thinks of Good it is easy to behave well, but when he misbehaves it is the Evil that a person seriously thinks about as concerns his life."

Jim closed his eyes and let the words caress him. They were Delaware words, and then he contrasted them with other words he had heard from a white preacher with froth practically coming from his mouth as he screamed, "I tell you that you're going to burn in Hell. You're going to suffer so much you'll scream for forgiveness, but there won't be any forgiveness. It'll be too late then. God has given you your chance! Do you want to be tortured forever, *eternally*, in hellfire? Christ Jesus can help you now, but if you turn your back on Him, *He will turn His back on you!*"

Jim shuddered. The frenzy of wild men who pretend to be civilized! He flipped the pages to find the words of Black Hawk: "We can only judge of what is proper and right by our standard of what is right and wrong, which differs widely from the whites, if I have been correctly informed. . . . The whites may do wrong all their lives and then if they are sorry for it when about to die, all is well, but with us it is different. We must continue to do good throughout our lives."

Jim looked up at the library wall where a picture of President Dwight Eisenhower was hanging. It seemed to say, "Give up, Indian! We're running the show now!" But Jim turned away and grinned to himself. "Go to hell, Ike! I've found this library and I'm going to unlock what it has in it. I'm not going to end up a drunk. Oh no, I'm gonna see if there isn't another way to deal with this racist society. I may never get to be a president like you, but maybe I'll find something better to be! An Indian!"

MY FATHER'S VISIT

"JACK, WHERE ARE YOU? I'M COMING TO GET YOU."

My father's voice sent me into a panic. I couldn't see him, being at the other end of the house, but I knew he was angry. Why? I couldn't guess. I just panicked. Some unexplainable fear took hold and before he could get to me, I was out of the house, slipping loosely out the door. Lightly, without making any noise, I ran down the back steps, down the driveway, and out to the street.

I ran desperately along the neighboring houses, thinking all the time. Where to hide? What to do? I needed a plan. But finally instinct took me along a path at right angles, and I slipped behind a thick wall of bushes. He would never see me there.

I had had a lot of practice at jungle and mountain warfare when playing as a child. That helped me in situations like this. I knew how to disappear into shrubbery, or under a house, or into a side canyon.

I felt in my pockets. Good! Without conscious planning I had picked up my pipe, tobacco, and matches. No telling how long I might be away. And money? Yes, I had enough. But I couldn't smoke now. He might notice it in the air.

Through the bushes I saw him coming. He was looking for me. His face looked tired and I felt sorry for him for some reason. I wanted to go out to him, but I was afraid.

After he had gone past, I got out from behind the

bushes and, running, retraced my steps back to the house.

I went in and sought out my mother. I said, "Why is Daddy chasing me? What does he want? He seems angry. What did I do?"

She looked at me strangely. Tears were in her eyes. She said, "Daddy is not feeling good." She broke down. "He feels very ill—not just a sickness. He says he's going to die soon . . . and he wants to play with you, to do something with you, while he still can." She was crying.

All kinds of deep feelings flooded through my mind. I turned and ran outside to find him.

I ran and I ran, but before I could find him I woke up.

In the dark room, a room so different from my childhood bedroom, I reached for my pipe and to-bacco. I smoked and saw my father's face. He was kind-looking but tired. In a few more years would I look the same?

He had gone to sleep almost thirty years before. I had helped put him in the earth. Someday I will catch up with him, I thought. Someday I will finish that dream . . . and we will play together like he wanted.

THE PROFESSOR

A NORTH AMERICAN PROFESSOR, AN AUTHOR OF SCHOL-
arly books and articles, was very deeply affected by
the predictions being made in the late 1970s to the
effect that nuclear war would be inevitable unless people became involved in a vigorous peace movement.
He was especially alarmed by Pentagon estimates of a
50 percent probability of war by 1985.

Not surprisingly perhaps, he abandoned his regular research to undertake a great deal of reading rela-
tive to the subject. He learned, among other facts, that
the entire northern half of the globe would be utterly
destroyed. He also discovered that prevailing air currents during much of the year would also endanger
the Southern Hemisphere, with the exception of New
Zealand, Pitcairn Island, and Antarctica.

After a great deal of thought, the professor decided
to reorient his priorities. He dropped his normal research and concentrated on making contact with a major library in Christchurch, New Zealand. There he
established a special collection in his own name where
his books, articles, manuscripts, correspondence, and
diaries could be safely preserved for posterity.

Then, deeply relieved, he resumed his old apoliti-
cal pattern of life with renewed vigor.

SOUTHSIDE

"YOU HAVE BEEN ASSIGNED TO A VERY IMPORTANT JOB, Grimes. As you know, this work requires more than just the highest level of security clearance. It, above all else, requires a deep sense of loyalty—absolute, undivided loyalty—to the principles on which our civilization is based. You have been judged to have these characteristics.

"You are now working for an agency that has no name. It is coordinated through the National Security Office, but only a handful of people know of its existence, and, in fact, the people working for it receive their salaries from a variety of sources. We call it the Interagency Contingency Planning Unit, or IACPU, but more commonly, for reasons you will soon comprehend, we also call it Southside.

"The fact that you served as a Mormon missionary in Argentina and that your Spanish is excellent means that you can proceed immediately to your other language assignment. For two weeks you will receive intensive training in Afrikaans, and then you will be sent to South Africa for eight weeks. There you will perfect your language ability as well as study, in great depth, various aspects of the economy, politics, and defense strategy of the RSA. You will work closely with your counterparts there.

"When not studying, you will have a chance to read a little novel that I'm going to give you."

"Sir, did you say a novel?"

The officer laughed out loud. "Yes, a novel. A work of fiction, but—and you will soon realize this—a secret novel whose plot is the basis for your assignment. This book is printed in such a way that it will disappear with exposure to sunlight. It must be destroyed after you have digested its contents."

William Grimes left the building in a state of quiet satisfaction. He felt that at long last his training in political science and public administration would be put to good use as an important part of the struggle to preserve Christian civilization.

He glanced up at the building. It was a shabby-looking one in a rundown section of the district, but the facade was deceiving. The offices inside were extremely modern and outfitted with the latest in electronic gadgetry.

Bill Grimes was used to facades. He had been recruited from BYU into the FBI and had served in that agency for five years. Then he had worked for the CIA for two years, in both cases frequently working out of phony fronts in both the USA and South America. Now, officially, he was to be assigned to the South World Trading Corporation, a company with unknown ownership but one having close connections with influential groups in Argentina, Chile, and South Africa.

Grimes read a little of the novel (called *South Option*) every day in between his Afrikaans training. Finally he completed the book and sat spellbound, thrilled and yet shocked by the story.

"Wow. I can't believe what I've read—and yet, it's all so logical, so well worked out. Some of the boys in the company must have put it together."

Bill reviewed, in his own mind, the basic theses of the book: first, that experts had determined that a nuclear war was inevitable, with a 50 percent probability by 1985 and a 99 percent probability by the early 1990s; second, that the Northern Hemisphere would be destroyed and that neither shelters nor any other procedure could possibly serve to reduce the destruction to manageable levels.

Bill opened the book to locate a key passage:

Western Europe and North America will be totally destroyed, along with the USSR and Japan. The Caucasian race will be 90 percent exterminated. The capitalist–free enterprise world will be devastated. Depending on the direction of air currents at the time, the near-Caucasians and part-Caucasians of the middle portions of the globe will also be wiped out by means of radiation sickness. Only the southernmost parts of the world have a reasonable survival probability.

Our proposition is this: we can afford to destroy the USSR or China only if we can find a way to ensure the survival of enough Caucasians and Christians to guarantee that the blacks, Indians, Native Americans, and Pacific peoples are not able to dominate the Safe Zones. As the situation now stands, the blacks and mixed people are a large majority in South Africa, while in the region from Argentina to Australia the white race is a majority. On the other hand, many Chileans are of nonwhite race, and survivors from Bolivia and Paraguay might seriously dilute the largely Caucasian character of Argentina and Uruguay. Moreover, the safest regions (extreme southern Patagonia) are underpopulated and largely nonwhite or mixed.

The plan that has been developed is really quite simple. We will secretly colonize as many white Americans as possible in Patagonia, South Africa, New Zealand, Tasmania, and Australia. We will especially select people from among those groups most loyal to capitalism and white patriotism, i.e., fundamentalist Protestants, Mormons, German Catholics, and so on.

By 1990 we hope to transfer ten million Caucasians to South Africa, twenty million to South America, and ten million to Australia, Tasmania, and New Zealand. Still further, by that date scientific and engineering procedures will make possible the colonization of Antarctica by perhaps ten thousand initial colonists.

He paused in his reading and then went ahead to a different section focusing on the economy:

By the mid-1980s the leading U.S. corporations and banks had already succeeded in establishing significant beachheads in the Southern Hemisphere, with a great deal of capital permanently transferred. By 1990 the United States had ceased, in fact, to be a major manufacturing center or holder of capital, except on paper. The largest corporations had begun to shift their centers of operations to safe areas in South Africa and elsewhere. Vast quantities of gold, uranium, aluminum, and other essential resources were stockpiled in caverns in Patagonia and Antarctica.

The takeover of the governments of the south was, of course, accomplished easily. The assassination of Allende in Chile marked the end of any problems in South America. South Africa was already a key participant and fully cooperative. It was determined to leave Australia and New Zealand intact as their white-oriented governments were firm allies of the United States in any case. . . .

The largest corporations and government power centers began, in 1983, to send their key executives on frequent visits to the South Zone. Thus, at the very least, a large portion would be able to take command after the nuclear exchange was completed. The most important owners of capital developed homes in Safe Zones. . . .

Every move was carried out with great secrecy and caution. Only the Inner Group was aware of the Option. The president was, of course, not a part of the Inner Group, since the latter consisted only of the corporate and defense elite. It was hoped, however, that he could be rescued from his White House shelter and command center.

The world was largely devastated by the Third World War. Almost two billion persons died; however, the United States was reorganized immediately in the South Zone, with its capital at Tierra del Fuego. The line of approximate safety ran through north-central Australia to northern Chile and Argentina and through southern Zimbabwe. Approximately one hundred million Caucasians survived, along with forty million nonwhites. The latter were relocated outside of the Safe Zones. . . . Christian civilization had survived and everyone looked forward to the day when the earth could be repeopled with a homogeneous population of enterprising, pioneering settlers. Already scientists were hard at work on a radiation-proof mobile environment to be used in the reclamation process, according to press releases from Johannesburg.

Grimes exposed the book to the sun and destroyed it.

Bill Grimes, his wife, their children, and near in-laws were among those colonized in Argentina. But when the nuclear exchange occurred, Grimes was on detached duty at an underground center in mid-Antarctica where secret nuclear missile silos had been carved out. It was jokingly called China Station, because its warheads were targeted toward south China and Southeast Asia, just in case the communists in those regions survived the Third World War. Grimes had been transferred to a task force planning the Fourth World War, designed to deal with that eventuality.

For several days the workers at China Station received war bulletins from New Zealand, but then all outside contact was broken off. No radio stations were broadcasting anywhere, it seemed. Supply planes stopped coming. China Station had a three-month supply of food.

The different bases in Antarctica managed to maintain contact with each other by radio so long as electric power was generated. But eventually all fuel had to be reserved for heating purposes only.

After thirty-six days the last fuel ran out in the last base.

The world was silent.

WHEN PROFESSORS DIE

HOW MUCH TIME WAS LEFT? A FEW SECONDS?

Only minutes, at the most. Maybe only a heartbeat and then it would be all over. In the utter darkness I kissed her lips, felt her body against mine. She was quiet, waiting.

I stroked her hair, squeezed her tightly, listening to the soft, hissing sound close by.

For some reason I smiled to myself. Here I was, thirty years old and yet I couldn't remember anything except what had occupied the last hour or so. Somehow my life had become compressed, even as the darkness now pressed in on me. My life was compressed spatially to this little washroom and temporally to these last few moments.

Was it the pain? Did I have to kill the memory of the death of all of those whom I loved, in fact, the death of everything? A healing insanity, compassionate amnesia? Is that what it was?

An hour earlier I had been attending a meeting upstairs in the School of Education offices. I couldn't recall too much, except that we were listening to the controversial theories of Doctor Chamberlain Stoddard, a professor who was trying to prove that blacks and Indians had lower IQs than whites and that our inferiority was permanent, genetically based.

And yet I could recall some of my comments. Of course, I had argued that Stoddard's white, black, and Indian populations were not genuine groups but were, in fact, simply arbitrary agglomerations of genetically, culturally, and socially distinct aggregates. But the thing that stuck in my mind now was what one Chicano colleague had said: "Doctor Stoddard, would there be more or less genocide and mass murder and torture in the world if we eliminated people with high IQ scores or low IQ scores? What about El Salvador and Guatemala and Argentina and South Africa, Professor? Do we know the IQ scores of those who have unleashed terror like a wild beast upon us?"

Stoddard chose to ignore all such soft arguments. "Science will solve all of our problems. We must use quantitative science. Emotional considerations should be set aside. Cold, dispassionate science . . ."

The phrase "Science will solve all of our problems" ran through my head.

"God, how strange this is!" I muttered. Here I was in a different city from the one in which I lived. Fate, like a razor-sharp knife, had severed my life into two parts. Now there was only the before that I had cast aside and the after that was still sharp and clear.

My life began—my present life—when I accepted the inevitability of my impending death and started to live with the rhythm of my death song.

My memory began retracing the events of my new life—the one that had commenced less than an hour before. I was sitting with other professors in the seminar room when a secretary outside started screaming. We all jumped up and rushed out to see what was wrong. People were already running through halls and offices with fear masking their faces.

"It just came over the intercom—and on the radio— we're about to be destroyed—nuclear missiles are on their way—our missiles have been fired—bombers are in the air—my children are still at school—oh, God!"

Sirens had started screaming. Everyone was running toward the stairways or trying to pack into over-loaded elevators.

I could feel the adrenaline surge through my body, and I began to panic also. But then I caught myself. What was there to do? Death was certain. My home was far away. There was no way I could reach it. I couldn't do anything for anybody except those nearby.

I picked up a phone and tried to call my mother in a distant city. No use. The phones were all busy or out of order. Probably the phone employees had all abandoned their offices.

What to do? I thought back to the teachings of the elders, of Black Elk and Lame Deer, of Don Juan and the ancient poems of the Aztecs. The moments of death are precious. One must not panic. Whatever time I have left belongs only to me now. I must use it well.

I saw a familiar secretary leaning against a door frame, as if exhausted. She was a young brown woman I had admired before. "Arenda, what do we do now?" I said quietly. "Oh, God!" she replied, putting her arms out toward me. I took them and pulled her close.

"I can't do nothin'," she sobbed. "My folks are too far away. I can't get to 'em in time. I just don't know what to do. Those goddamn sons of bitches in the Pentagon . . . and the Kremlin, too. . . . They're killin' all of us."

"Yeah, I know. It looks like they're gonna kill off the whole white race and we just got caught in the middle. . . . They're all gonna be dead, Arenda, just like us. . . . Anyway, listen, I haven't got anybody either."

I hugged her tightly. "Why don't we go someplace and be together. That would be better than just cryin' and a lot better than killin'. Besides, I've always wanted to tell you that you're a fantastic-lookin' woman."

"You crazy Indian! I always wondered how *you*

could be a professor. You didn't have books on your mind all the time, huh?"

We decided to go down to the basement of the building. Arenda said there were a lot of rooms down there.

Just as we were going into a big storage room underground, I spotted Professor Stoddard.

He was crouched against a wall, fear written all over his face. He was shaking and as I passed by I could smell the odor of human feces. He couldn't control his organs and a pool of urine had collected where he was huddled.

I had never talked to the man individually before, mostly out of fear that I would lose my temper, but now some compulsion drew me toward him. Just then a black graduate student shouted, "Professor Stoddard, you've always argued that we nonwhites are intellectually inferior. Okay, what's the IQ of the bastards setting off these missiles? Is this the final genocide carried out by your superior Western civilization?"

He looked at us in stark terror, but he appeared to understand the question.

"Doctor Stoddard, I want to know something? Who dies easier? A man with a high IQ or a man with a low IQ?"

The onetime arrogant professor turned away to retch on the wall. I didn't feel sorry for him, however, because I knew that men of his same mentality and hard, cold insensitivity had planned the deaths of all of us.

"Professor, how do you quantify compassion? How do you quantify love? Can you measure arrogance? Can you measure greed on one of your tests? . . . Doctor, I ask you again: are these members of the IQ superrace who have brought us to this?"

Arenda had been looking on with disbelief. But

now she started laughing, rather hysterically I thought, and then shouted at the trembling, heaving academic, "I always thought you were a big pile of shit, *Doctor* Stoddard. Now you can use your studies of all those IQs to wipe up your own vomit!"

The good professor was now gagging on his own bile and we left, but the grad student got off one parting shot: "Tell me, Professor, do high IQ or low IQ people suffer less from radioactive poisoning . . . or from radiation burns. Shall we see? Shall we get everybody's IQ score down here and then do a study after this is all over? You can become famous . . . in hell!"

Finally I said, "The Creator will judge your work doctor and that of all your colleagues from Moscow to Los Alamos!"

Most of the people in the basement were huddled against walls, with blank faces and staring eyes. Some were praying. Some were quietly moaning. A few were shrieking. I took Arenda's hand and together we began investigating all of the hallways, closets, and laundry rooms. Finally we located a supply and wash room, where there were some gas-fired hot water heaters. We went in to wait, alone, away from the others.

"There are two things I want to do now. I want to pray for all living things and I want to be close to you. I want our deaths to be as beautiful as possible and . . . well, I want to die in touch with someone, because that's a prayer, too."

We both prayed for those whom we loved, for the beautiful earth, for the trees and plants, for all living things. We were angry at what the U.S. government had done to us in the name of a defense that was really only mass murder. But we gradually cleansed ourselves of hate and bitterness and reached a state of strange calmness.

I shut off the gas valves, turned off all the lights, and began holding her close. At that moment all hell broke loose. Warheads began hitting the area. The noise was deafening, beyond comprehension, and the building shook as if an earthquake was under way. We could hear walls or floors and ceilings collapsing and glass shattering . . . and people screaming.

But we didn't surrender to terror. Driven by an elemental force, we desperately loved each other, seeking through the magic and power of love to give birth to a counterbalance to all of the evil unleashed by obstinate madmen.

And somehow we lived through that first attack. Our room remained intact. Still, we knew that there was no escape from death; we were without food, without a permanent supply of clean air, and with no place to go even if we could have gotten out of our sanctuary. And we did not want to see the melted faces, the running eyes, the burned bodies, the severed limbs.

And so we lay there, naked, caressing each other and talking of love and of the next life, and of what we would say to our loved ones when we met them, and of the Indian prophecies.

"We are all just a part of the Great Mystery. Now we are going to experience a transformation. We are shedding skins. But the Great Mystery, which is us, will go on."

Finally, in a period of rest, Arenda said, "I want to go now. I'm ready to die. I don't want to wait any longer. I can hear the fires getting closer."

I could also feel the increasing heat generated by fires somewhere outside of our room. I reached in the darkness for the gas jets and turned them all on.

As we lay together, there, in love, death crept up around us, hissing softly.

THE DREAM OF INJUN JOE

A Page from the
Alcatraz Seminars

DEAR READER: I WAS INDEED FORTUNATE TO BE ALIVE IN 1969–1970 and to be able to join the throngs of Native Americans visiting or living on Alcatraz Island in those exciting days. For those too young to remember, I will provide only this background: for several years that sad rock in the Bay of San Francisco, long the locale of a notorious prison, was liberated from its forlorn destiny by Indians from many tribes. For a brief time, then, the Isla de los Alcatraces knew a different existence, one filled with the sounds of drumming, singing, laughter, and angry but proud speeches.

I remember very distinctly my impressions: the blueness of the bay dotted with little boats of every description making their way to the miniature island; the happy faces of the native people, long black hair tied back with red headbands; the put-putting of ancient motors in old boats whose seaworthiness was open to doubt; and the fog banks courteously holding themselves out to sea, allowing the sun to have a few hours of dominion.

One thing that especially struck me was how the U.S. government had spent great sums of money to build and maintain a massive prison on the island, only to be ultimately—and inevitably—defeated by the intrepid and natural liberators of salt and water, fog and wind.

And I thought to myself, "Thus it will be! All the might and wealth of the United States cannot prevent its ultimate decay." It seemed as if natural law had led the Indians to Alcatraz, to begin a process of rebirth amid the visible signs of rusting cell doors and decaying barred windows.

"We must become like the salt and the waters of the earth. We must slowly, but certainly, rust away this prison erected all around us."

But enough of my personal feelings! What I want to recount, dear reader, is the nature of the intellectual life that developed on the island in those days, and, more especially, I wish now to recount, as faithfully as I can from my extensive notes, the precise content of one of the now legendary Alcatraz seminars.

The colloquium commenced when a Cherokee scholar named Marshall (I can't recall whether this was his first or last name) asked and then answered a rhetorical question: "How can we describe the character of the whites who came over here from Europe, especially the negative traits that caused so much trouble?

"What is it that dominates their character?

"It isn't just materialism, nor is it just greed—what makes many white people so strange and so dangerous is a restless dissatisfaction that is constant, never satisfied. They are crazy for wealth, voracious. They will go to any lengths, go to any place, use any means, to get what they want.

"In less than a century they have consumed most of the United States' oil and gas reserves, reserves that took millions of years to accumulate.

"They have wiped out forests, destroyed grasslands, turned deserts into dust bowls, and seriously diminished almost every other natural resource. What are their characteristics? Igana-noks-salgi. Those who are greedy for land, the old Creek Indians called them. They are always gobbling up land, taking it from Indians, Mexicans, or less successful white people.

"They are always looking for gold, for uranium, for oil, for more profits, for new real estate deals, for better-paying jobs, for a new place to live.

"In truth, it is not wealth that they want; it is always *more wealth* or *new* wealth.

"It is not so much *having* something but *getting* something that drives them. If they already have, they want to get more—always more." He paused for a moment, staring up at the high prison ceiling with its bare patches where plaster and paint had fallen away.

"They are crazy—driven, restless, dissatisfied—but it is *to get* that they are crazy. Of course, many are crazy to spend, to display, to show off, but this need for consumption only serves to make the *getting* all the more important.

"They are crazy with the *getting* of wealth, the *getting* of land, the *getting* of gold, the *getting* of a new car, the *getting* of a chance to spend the way the Hollywood stars spend or the way the oil-rich Texas millionaires spend.

"Since they are Getting-Crazy People, they seldom enjoy merely *having.* This is the root of their restless character. This is why they plunder Lake Tahoe, the Sierra Nevada foothills, the Arizona desert, the Colorado Rockies, and so on. They want *to get* a place at the beach, or on the lake, or in the desert. They don't care that one of the consequences of their getting such a place will be the destruction of that very place.

"It is not the having but the getting! After the place bores them or is destroyed, they can *get* some other place. So what else is new?

"Maybe this is also why some of them chase after religious cults in such a relentless, frenetic, capitalistic way. They have a need not to *have* a spiritual life but to *get* some kind of experience. Many will try dozens of techniques, cults, and formulas, different brands to be consumed and tossed aside."

He paused and someone asked him, "What do we do with them?" Many people smiled or laughed to themselves.

"What do you do with them? For one thing, it's no good to set up a communist society. The Getting-Crazy People will shrewdly figure out that they can still wheel and deal. Sure, they will join the party! They will work their way up to leadership positions and become a new ruling class, getting new cars, new apartments, country estates, privileges of all kinds, just as in Russia. Or some will become scientists or technicians and join the technical-bureaucratic new rich.

"What can you do with them? They create a world of pornography, dancing naked girls, selling sex as a commodity, motels with piped-in X-rated movies, waterbeds, and vibrators, prostitution, Las Vegas, Reno, Tijuana, Gay Paree. Get some sex! Buy it! Sell it! Soon every house (maybe offices, too, and subway stations) will have robot crawl-in sex machines right next to the washer and dryer or the soft-drink dispensers. Psychologists will endorse the machines (it will protect young women, diminish sexual aggression)."

Discussion then ensued on this point for a while but soon shifted back to an anthropology of white people. Marshall had a great many stimulating thoughts, not surprising for an Indian who had studied at the Sorbonne and had written plays in Cherokee.

"Right now the Alcatraz Nation is negotiating with white bureaucrats and a political appointee of the vice-president. What do you know about any of them? What do I know? What kind of people are they? It is highly likely that they are a part of, or at least work for, the Getting-Crazy culture I spoke of before.

"I'm not just talking about studying gun-carrying KKKers, or Nazis, or white vigilante groups. I'm not just talking about studying holy rollers or rattlesnake handlers. I'm talking about studying the Kissingers, Bundys, Rostows, Nixons, Erlichmans, and Johnsons, in short, the ruling class of leadership in this society."

That particular gathering also included an Iroquois young man who, although completely traditional in appearance, had traveled widely and was always setting forth deep thoughts. He rose and began speaking:

"Let's get back to the question of what can be done with white people. We may not have the power to *do* anything, but I have learned a lot about the study of Europeans by just dealing with the question.

"I'll tell you what. Let me describe an Indian and his ideas, or maybe I should say fantasies. Since my name is Joe, I'll call him Injun Joe. They could be my own daydreams, but I'll just say that they belong to Injun Joe, since I know they are shared by other fantasizers among us.

"Now this Injun Joe often daydreamed. Sometimes he would go back in time, in the spaceship of his mind, to the days of Osceola, one hundred thirty years ago, when the Seminoles and their black allies were fighting for the simple right to have a homeland. The Seminoles, Miccosukees, and their allies were great fighters, but Joe knew that there were too few Indians to defeat the whites in Florida. The available manpower could never be sufficient both to wage offensive warfare and to defend liberated zones. Joe's strategy was therefore to organize a large assault force that would trap and cut to pieces the major enemy units without, however, holding any territory. It would remain a mobile force, striking at will, disarming whites everywhere, but not setting up any garrisons. Its major purpose, after eliminating U.S. units in Florida, was to strike deep into Georgia, toward the Guale coast, in order to free and arm thousands of the slaves.

"Joe was able to recruit several thousand Creeks, mixed-bloods, and freed slaves to join his main force. Rapidly this unit was supplemented by armed slave armies organized in Georgia. In this manner the white settlers in Florida, cut off on the north and mostly disarmed, were forced to flee to fortified positions. It was now they who were on the defensive; while the liberation armies were free to probe into Alabama and central Georgia.

"The U.S. government was caught off guard by the loss of its invading units in Florida, and this provided the liberation forces with the chance to move tens of thousands of freed slaves into Florida.

"Gradually, armed liberation units, using captured artillery pieces, were able to capture all of the invaders' positions in Florida (which was now called the Republic of Bimini). To the north, meanwhile, the slave population was rebelling throughout Georgia and Alabama, with guerrilla units spreading also into South Carolina.

"In the meantime, Joe had set up an effective system of sending news bulletins to newspapers in Boston, New York, and Philadelphia. By this means it became clearly established in people's minds that the war was nothing more or less than a struggle between slave-owner imperialism, on the one hand, and freedom and justice, on the other. Would New England and the North support a war to crush the Indians and other nonwhite people in order to advance the interests of the slave-owning classes?

"Joe knew that it didn't matter. The freedom fighters could get some help from New England, but the problem still remained that the slavocracy ran the federal government and that tens of thousands of whites from

Kentucky, Tennessee, North Carolina, and so on would enroll in the militia in order to crush the hated red and brown and black niggers (and in order to get a chance at bounty land).

"The Bimini strategy was to remove all Indian and other nonwhite women and children of color from South Carolina, northern Georgia, and Alabama and send them either to Bimini itself or to safe regions in Guale and along the Appalachee River. Northern Georgia and Alabama were to serve as a no-man's-land buffer zone where whites were disarmed but otherwise left alone (most fled north) and where slavery ceased to exist.

"Another element in the Bimini strategy was to send out spies to locate places where the white governments were assembling militia units or stockpiling arms. These areas were then hit by mobile assault forces before the state troops were prepared or organized. A similar strategy was followed as regards the organizing of U.S. regular forces.

"The Bimini intelligence system was quite good. It had to be, since the freedom forces were the weaker party and their success hinged entirely upon preventing any large army from being fully organized.

"Gradually, as the ex-slaves and free Indians became more experienced and confident, and as thousands were armed with liberated weapons, it became possible to launch major rapid assaults into the tidewater of southside Virginia, north Carolina, and other areas where the slaves numbered more than half of the population. Guerrilla units were organized in many areas as the war zone expanded.

"Anyway, this was one of Joe's dreams. This one, like most of them, came up against some hard realities. What do you do with white people if you defeat them militarily? Joe was not about to adopt the white value system of enslavement and genocide. Still, many of the whites would be just as aggressive and villainous after conquest as before. They would scheme and plot and try to find ways to recover their lost empire. They were experienced at politics and knew how to organize. Few could be trusted.

"Joe hit on one plan: to divide up the rich planters' estates among poor and landless whites as well as among the ex-slaves. But would that really work? Would the poor whites appreciate having small farms of their own, or would they listen to the slave owners' propaganda of white racial superiority and unity?

"And, of course, another problem was, would the U.S. government *ever* agree to allow Indians and other nonwhites to be free and independent? Could the USA ever tolerate a brown victory, or would it keep recruiting new white armies, one after another, to try to crush the injuns and niggers (even if this meant a war of genocidal intensity and ever-expanding character)?

"Joe realized that by the 1830s and 1840s it was too late for a real Indian victory. The whites were just too numerous. White families had ten or twelve children every generation, the women being little more than walking (working) incubators. Indian families usually had only three or four children, and many died because of always being pressed to the wall by constant white aggression. The slave birthrate was higher than that of the Indian, but it, too, was being overwhelmed by the constant flood of European immigrants. In any case, the slaves were usually terrorized systematically and prevented from learning about things essential for effective rebellions.

"Joe's dreams often focused on earlier times, before the U.S. war for independence, for example, or he would shift the locale to Mexico. Sometimes Joe's great Indian alliance system was able to defeat the white colonial settlers, free the slaves, and establish a benign federal democracy (patterned after the Iroquois League). But the problem still remained—what to do with white people.

"If you had five-hundred thousand, or a million, or two million whites under your control, how could you change their culture so that they would stop trying to get more wealth all of the time? And they reproduced so fast that if you didn't watch out, they would be flooding into Indian regions by sheer numbers.

"Indian people traditionally are brought up to live in a democracy. They don't need big government, prisons, police, zoning commissions, investigative bodies, or things like that. They have small families and raise their children to be polite and observant, worship the Creator, and respect each other. So you could have a very loose confederacy insofar as Indians are concerned.

"But what can you do with a million (or more) restless, aggressive, materialistic, scheming, proliferating white people who like to break laws, don't respect other people, and consider themselves to be the New Israelites, God's chosen people, destined to get whatever they want?

"That's a real dilemma, isn't it? Now, old Injun Joe realized that that was why the USA was not, and probably could never be, a democracy. Indians can live in freedom. Whites have to be controlled, or they will even exploit each other. So every white state has to have a big government. If it doesn't, factory owners will enslave their workers, manufacturers will cheat (or poison) their customers, land speculators will get control of all of the good land, railroads will charge whatever the traffic will bear, and the earth, water, and air will be raped, scraped, looted, and polluted.

"Of course, white people also have had big governments to help control slaves and to even invent (or at least okay) the idea that free Indians and Africans can be captured or bought and kept in chains forever from that day forth.

"So what do you do with them? Nobody knows. That's what the problem with U.S. politics is today, right now. The president doesn't know; he's one of them!

"So, anyway, what is Injun Joe going to do with white people in his dreams, in his fantasies? He's got them defeated, let's say, but how can he change them enough so that they can live in a democracy? Joe toyed with the idea of establishing Indian garrisons to control the whites and a totally Indian-run colonial administration to supervise them. But that idea bothered him. That's just what whites do to Indians.

"The bad thing about it, Joe thought, is that if native people had to have standing armies, police, and colonial officials to control the whites, they would have to change their own way of life to do so. What happened to the Mongols, the Manchus, the Turks, the Arabs, the Macedonians, the Greeks, the Romans? Injun Joe had studied history enough to know that ultimately empires enslave the victors as much as the defeated. He could not imagine a Black Elk, or a Tecumseh, or a Sitting Bull, or a Geronimo sitting around giving orders to white people, watching them, becoming fat and lazy off of other people's work. Indians were free, because they let others be free. Many white people were slaves to their own systems of exploitation. Sure, he thought, the rulers can have all of the luxuries they want, but that only whets their appetites; they can have any slave woman they want, but that only corrupts their own natural sexuality, makes it into some kind of rape, the birth of sex as pornography.

"No, Indians must win, *but they cannot rule*, because to rule is to become a slave to the evil passions that come with secular power. The white people must be free, but how?

"Injun Joe's dreams led him to the conclusion that the only means available was to divide up the land in the liberated areas in such a way that every rural family, white, mixed, or black, had at least a forty-acre farm. These farms would be given out in such a manner that most areas would have blacks and browns mixed in with whites. Of course, the whites would outnumber the nonwhites about three to one overall, but during a transition period the former slave owners and other exploitative classes would be prohibited from holding office. Schools and colleges would favor nonwhite enrollment, and no whites could bear arms.

"Joe fantasized that immigration from Haiti, Mexico, and other nonwhite areas might gradually help increase the brownness of the race mixture, and cultural borrowing might blunt the hard edges of the European character. The result might be something like a Brazil or a Puerto Rico, a land full of mixed people but, and this was the big one, without the political oppression resulting from the uninterrupted economic and political power of white elites and the uninterrupted poverty and ignorance of the brown masses.

"Utopia, you say? A land of mixed-bloods in North America guided toward democracy by wise native guardians. Could it ever be? Could it ever have been?

"But Joe's dreams were not too far-fetched. Right there in Oklahoma, before 1890, it was happening in the Muscogee Creek Republic, and it happened in the Seminole Republic as well. Indians, blacks, whites, red-blacks, mulattoes, half-breeds, you name it, living together, intermarrying, sharing life, getting along, until the sacred treaties were broken and the white ruling class decided that brown people had no right to self-government anywhere in the territory of Yankee-Dixi-Doo. Paradise was plundered and terror replaced tolerance.

"What do you do with the Getting-Crazy People? If only they would leave you alone, or maybe they could find another planet (with lots of gold) and go there.

"In Joe's dreams there was always a place for good people of all races. He realized, in fantasy as in real life, that the majority of white people were not bad, that they were also victims. He tried in his dreams to fantasize ways that Indians could somehow communicate with these silent white people.

"He never found a way."

For a long time there was nothing but silence in the seminar. All of the people just sat there looking inward, vibrations of Injun Joe filling the room.

Marshall broke the silence: "Do Indians have dreams? You bet we do! How else could we have survived all these years?

"The white people have never known of our dreams, our fantasies. They think Indians just sit, staring into space, from the top of a mesa somewhere.

"Our dreams belong to us. Now the time has come to share them with each other and to see what we can do with them."

SOUTH OF HOPE

HE WATCHED INTENTLY AS A CAR MADE ITS WAY ALONG the dirt road, raising a cloud of dust. Smokelike, the dust rose up several dozen feet into the air and then slowly drifted toward the south, dropping back to the earth gradually.

The car passed by a hundred yards away and Emory breathed more deeply. It was only then he became aware that he had been holding his breath. "How long can we stay here, cooped up like this?" he thought.

There were seven of them in that house, not counting the graduate student and his wife and their baby. It was crowded and they couldn't even go outside except at night.

He rested his hands on the shovel and looked up at the stars. The dry night air sucked up his sweat, cooling him as it did so.

"How much more are we going to dig? This hole is big enough to hold all the food you can ever raise!"

"Almost done! Just a little bit more and we'll cover it up with timbers and earth."

"It'll be a good storage cellar."

"Maybe a bomb shelter."

"Maybe a man and woman shelter!"

The graduate student and his wife were fixing up an old, rundown farm. By way of repayment for their generosity, the guests were doing what they could to help.

"It's good to be out here digging. I get so tense sometimes. You know, a person could go crazy just hiding."

Later they listened to the late news on the radio, news mostly about the success of the government in rounding up subversives and about plots and threats that made still more roundups necessary.

They sat around silently for a while, each one wrapped up in a lonely, separate world, pierced only by the glow of a cigarette here and there.

"I wonder what's happened to Ed White Deer? I wonder if he's still alive. They got him in the first roundup, ya know," thought Emory out loud.

"It sounds terrible, but what I was just thinking about is how long the university will keep on depositing our paychecks in the bank now that we're gone. My wife and kids won't have any food or a roof over their heads before long. I guess she'll have to get a job—if she can find one—and they'll have to find a small flat or move in with someone else."

"Don't worry, Carl; they'll survive some way."

"Sometimes I wonder if I didn't run away too soon," said Al Gomez, a young Chicano assistant professor. "So far as I know there's still no warrant for my arrest. Maybe I just panicked. What do you think?"

"You did the right thing. You know as well as the rest of us that the first wave of arrests hit all of the community organizers, labor radicals, ethnic group leaders, left political types—all the people out in the barrios, on the streets, in the communities.

"The second roundup included all of the second level of organizers—professors with some record of radical activity included. That includes just about all of us. And it includes you. Do you think they don't know about your activity in MECHA, about your having been a Brown Beret a few years ago?"

"That's right. And now they're picking up all of the writers, broadcasters, journalists—anybody who might help keep the resistance going. Man, they've even arrested state legislators and congressmen!"

"Even a governor or two," commented Ann Suzuki, an organizer in the Asian community and a former lecturer.

A pause followed as Emory Six Towns passed some tobacco around. They had learned to roll their own cigarettes, those who smoked.

"Well, Carl, I know you've been predicting a military–right wing takeover for a long time. The good old USA gone the way of El Salvador and Guatemala! . . . How does it feel to have been proved right?"

"It don't feel good, man. It feels bad. . . . But, you know, even I was a little surprised. I mean, you know, the Democratic candidates won the election in a big way, and then, whammo, they blew our new president and vice-president away!"

"And then, dammit, they had the gall to blame it on left-wing terrorists, the sons of bitches!"

"If we get caught . . . I mean . . . do you think they're really torturing people?"

Silence crept into the circle until Emory said, "I ain't gonna get caught! . . . And that's one of the reasons! They've brought back troops from Central America and from the Canal Zone to help control us, to hunt us down. They've armed right-wing Cubans and Nicaraguans. Man! . . . These guys are the ones who have been encouraging torture everywhere from South Africa to South Korea. You think they're gonna just forget all of what they've taught everybody else?"

"I agree," said Professor Lester. "There's too much potential for a civil war. They've rounded up hundreds of thousands of people. Many of the inner cities and barrios have been in revolt. Potential rebels are everywhere. Only terror of the most extreme kind can ensure the takeover."

The graduate student, who was still able to travel about, added, "Rumor has it that they've armed the KKK and the Nazis. Many universities are totally shut down, and police and troops are at all of them, just like on our campus. It scares the shit out of me to go there. One of these days I may get cold feet and just not go back; it's that bad."

"Yes, but the majority of our dear colleagues are still just working away on their projects, not realizing that even they will one day be visited by the police!"

"Some of them—believe me—are very glad to see us gone. Now they don't have to worry about ethnic studies or about the teachers' union or about protests over the inhumane treatment of research animals! No . . . now they can get back to teaching the students how to memorize facts, how to be cogs in the system."

The hideaways took turns watching for strange vehicles by day and night. They listened to the radio frequently, just on the off chance that a dissident group might capture a station for a brief period. But authentic news was hard to come by. All over the country the situation was the same. Only the military and the right-wingers had access to reliable information.

"Orwell was just like an Indian, a real prophet. *1984* was a vision, not just a book."

Emory lay in the shade on cool, clean earth in a kind of a tunnel beneath a forest of trees and thick brush. He picked a tick off of his skin and started to break it in two between his fingernails. But then he just let it go.

His thoughts were wandering. No food for two days, no water for one. He noticed the dried blood on his arms, on the tops of his hands, but he looked away.

"Crawling, crawling. I must have crawled for miles."

The mountains were full of individuals and small groups hiding out as long as they had food, walking by night toward Canada. But the mountains were also full of soldiers, right-wing vigilantes, and secret police disguised as refugees.

This was no game. Those who were caught were killed on the spot or, if luck was against them, were taken away for interrogation.

Emory gripped his .22 rifle and started crawling again. He could smell the dampness of a little creek in a hollow just ahead.

"There were massive demonstrations in our city. Hundreds of thousands marched. But the soldiers and police moved in. They had the black and Chicano soldiers out in front, with white officers and other crackers behind them. The brothers shot over our heads, but the ofays didn't care. They mowed down thousands—men, women, children." His voice cracked.

"They've even arrested lots of minority soldiers or taken their guns away. I heard that some are fighting back, but I don't know where."

Emory didn't say anything at first. The black student didn't know about the mountains, didn't know how to get food. Emory felt a chill run through him. The young black man would never make it to Canada. He would die. Emory saw that.

He was filthy. He knew he looked filthy. He could smell his own body even above the smell of the pine forest. But he was sure now. He had crossed the border. Now he could rest, sleep, eat, fight for freedom, join the Canadians.

His mind whirled. He felt faint. He rose up, stretched his hands into the air.

An RCMP patrol saw him. Emory waved at them. Then he was lifted into the air as a beam of bullets tore into his stomach, cutting him in two.

He was lifted into the air, and he flew up high, and the Mounties grew smaller below him.

He thought he glimpsed the Arctic Ocean before a bluish-blackness covered everything over like a dense, heavy rain cloud.

THE SACRIFICE

"THROUGH THOSE MANY NIGHTS AND DAYS THEY TALKED endlessly. It was important, even crucial, that they consider the thing from every angle. And so they talked even though some ached from the effort to put off action when their bodies and minds were already at high tension, ready to spring like coiled snakes.

"The weather was good. The sun warmed them during the day without being too hot, and the nights were just cool enough to make the cook fire a source of needed warmth. The beauty of the place was reflected in the beauty of their hearts. The majesty of the lake, shimmering at dawn or at sunset, was reflected in the majesty of their purpose.

"Nestling on their mother's body, lying close to the earth or sitting on her, enjoying the warmth and softness of the soft, sandy soil—that's how they were. Feeling the slight breezes blowing off the lake, absorbing the closeness of the millions of stars in a sky devoid of the glare of artificial lights—there they were, about two dozen Indians, on their own mother land.

"This, my grandson, is how they felt at that time so long ago.

"I am going to tell you the truth about all these brave men and women, too, because I want you to know what kind of gift your own father left you.

"Your father was one of these dedicated ones. And now he is gone and cannot tell you himself about these things.

"I know that sometimes you miss your father. I know also that in your heart you maybe feel an ache, an aching that makes bitter thoughts. It's so hard for a young one to understand why fathers leave, why sometimes they have to go away, perhaps even die.

"But now I feel in *my* heart that it is time to tell you the real story so you will know what kind of a man your father, my son, was. And you will understand that he is with us still, in our hearts, in our minds, and that we shall see him again."

The old man looked up at the sky, tears almost flowing. Then he resumed talking once more.

"They were meeting on Indian land, in a clump of trees along a small creek not far from the shore of a beautiful lake. They were meeting far from white people, far from strange Indian visitors, and far from the lights of the white man's polluted 'civilization.'

"Their meeting was a secret one, a closed one, insofar as other humans were concerned. But it was open to the Great Creative Power, their Grandfather, and to all of his spirit children. They wanted to be close to the sacred soil of their mother, the earth, and close to their father, the sky. They needed at that time to be in their sacred church, the only Indian church, the church whose floor is earth and whose roof is sky. A church was needed, one not desecrated by evil.

"And so they met in a far corner of the Indian country, away from all other two-leggeds and away from the eyes and listening devices of the white man's society.

"No definite hour or day had been set for the meeting. They arrived in small groups or one by one. The first arrivals prepared the camp and built a sweat house near the lake shore, using old dead limbs for a framework erected over a little hollowed-out pit. Sweet-smelling living willow branches were woven in and out of the framework, and then earth and grass were used to make the roof almost airtight.

"As you know, Grandson, the sweat house was important. They felt the need to cleanse their bodies as well as their minds. Even as the white man's liquor was left behind, so, too, they needed to leave behind all evil thinking.

"Your father was one of these men, and all of those who were gathered together realized that they had to be pure. They intended to sacrifice their lives. They intended to die. They knew they would surely die before they saw another summer. They knew they had to be purified, as if they were going to take part in a holy ceremony. Indeed, they came to believe that theirs was a holy ceremony, a dance, not danced at one time or place but a dance nonetheless.

"They came from all over. They had seen many things. Some were educated. Some had never been to the white man's schools. Four were holy men, religious leaders. Some were old but strong; others were young and strong. All were prepared to die. Already they were thinking about their death songs, learning them well.

"I helped your father learn his song when you were so young and small, my grandson.

"Not all were men. Three were women who had brought their babies, because babies symbolized the life for their people that they were thinking on, and because these two-legged mothers wanted to be with their babies as long as they could. Soon these children would be raised by grandmothers, when the mothers were dead.

"So you can see how dedicated these ones, including your father, were, my grandson.

"Even mothers were willing to leave their babies—and that is a very hard thing for most women to do."

The boy was looking at the ground. He was listening intently to every word, but his eyes were focused on another world there on the ground, and in that world he could see the lake and everything his grandfather described.

The old man handed the boy a piece of dried meat to chew on. He said, "We are going to be here a long while. This story cannot be quickly told. So it is!

"The things I am going to tell you I observed myself or learned from one who survived for a time. It is all true what I am telling you, but, of course, there are still some things no one will ever know. A few things I cannot tell you yet, but they are not important at this time."

He paused and then went on.

"The elders and medicine people selected these men and women very, very carefully. They put them through many tests and watched each one for years. They knew that many Indians had become unreliable because of liquor and bad hearts. Some were even agents of the government, so the elders had to be extremely cautious. Thus it took a long time to prepare for the sacrifice.

"You can be very proud, as I am, that your father was among those chosen and that over many years he proved himself to be a true patriot, loyal to the Indian people in every way. Not only that, but he was judged to be intelligent and very calm in moments of crisis. That was as important as showing patriotism and being free of the use of drugs.

"As you can understand, an unstable person, especially one who cannot control his use of alcohol and drugs, is no good whatsoever in any serious undertaking.

"In any case, they met together and carefully prepared themselves spiritually. That was what they had to do. Oh, they also reviewed their plan of action, but it was the spiritual preparation that was essential.

"One of the medicine men had a dream there at that lake, and in that dream he saw many bodies dead or dying—Indians, that is—so he knew that all of them, or almost all, would give their lives. But he also saw that their sacrifice was necessary and that it would have a great impact."

The old man turned and looked to the sky, where the first evening star had appeared over the mountains.

"I must tell you also, although you may already know it, that the Indian nations had been trying for many, many years to get justice from the government. They had tried everything, petitions, peaceful demonstrations, legislation, protests, voting, everything. And it had all failed. The government just seemed intent on destroying the Indians. No appeals did any good. So what choice was left?

"The men and women who gathered at the lake were not violent people. No, just the opposite! They were religious, peaceful people. They didn't want to hurt anyone, and that is why they planned what they did.

"You see, many Indians and other poor people had become very bitter by that time. Some were ready to revolt, but, of course, that would do no good. They would just be crushed, wiped out. So these people, much like Jesus for the Christians, were ready to sacrifice themselves instead.

"Anyway, they gathered at the lake as I have described. Eventually there were seven times seven, or forty-nine. Everything had been planned out, and they were clean, ready to go.

"After that they left separately, and in different ways all made the journey to the capital of the government, where they hid out, preparing for the right moment.

"Part of the sacrificers, the elders mostly, had already arranged for an audience with the Big Man, el Presidente, the head of the white government, and with some other high officials. It had been arranged long before, and the old ones were going to the meeting in traditional clothing, with sacred prayers in their hearts but with weapons in their garments. They did not plan to kill anyone, but the weapons, they knew, were now the only things that that hypocritical white man would listen to. All talk had failed, not only with that Big Man but with others of the same kind before him.

"Everything went as planned. The guards and x-ray machines could not and did not learn about the Indians' purpose. Their weapons were undetectable, not being made of any metal, and their looks fooled the whites into complacency. The guards didn't realize that these old men were hard as nails and had been running and fasting for years in preparation for that day."

The grandfather stopped to pour a cup of coffee for himself, and the boy, after finishing a cold tortilla, asked, "Grandfather, how did it feel when they went in there? Did anyone tell you that? I mean what was it really like for them?"

The old man's eyes sparkled and he said, "Okay, I'll tell you the story in the words of one who was there and who lived for a little while afterward. And I will put in also what I myself saw when I went to the capital."

He paused and then went on, soon transfixed by a new mood taking hold of his emotions.

"Everybody went into this big meeting room, past lots of desks and secretaries. We all had calm faces, but our hearts were beating fast. Many hands were wet with sweat.

"Finally we all sat down and waited. First the high

officials came and then the leader himself. He was preoccupied with other business and was in a hurry. A smile was forced on his face, but we had only fifteen minutes, he said.

"Our plan worked well. Each elder went up to shake his hand and give him a gift. But the fourth elder had an extra something for him, a weapon, razor sharp, at his throat. And immediately the rest of us jumped into action, some surrounding the Big Man and others telling the guards, 'We are ready to die. We are prepared to kill your leader, but if you lay down your weapons no one will be hurt.'

"We had practiced this many times. Some things didn't go exactly as planned, but we adjusted to the changes.

"As soon as we had complete control of that big room and the surrounding offices, we forced the head security man to do the things we demanded: clear everyone else out of the entire building, leaving all of the guns and weapons behind, and allow one vehicle to pull right up next door. In that van were the rest of the forty-nine sacrificers with weapons and gas masks in case we needed them.

"The security people didn't want to leave, of course, but we were banking on the fact that they would be-lieve that we were ready to die right on the spot and to take the Big Man with us. So they finally obeyed our orders and cleared everybody out, leaving most of their guns and radios behind. We picked them all up and checked out the whole place, setting up our own guards at key places.

"The elders had everything carefully planned. We had people along who knew how to operate the radio equipment there as well as how to fix us all up in gas masks. We were worried, you see, about the govern-ment using gas to overcome us.

"Well, the first thing we did was to hide the Big Man in an easily defended set of inner rooms, with four tough men to guard him well. Then we got the radio room operating and went out on the air to tell the people why we were seizing the head of the government."

The grandfather, visibly sweating, paused for breath.

"You see, Grandson, everyone knew that many non-Indian people would be very upset, very angry at us. But that didn't matter! Everything else had been tried! Still, we had to try to get across the Indian's side of the story—why we were prepared to die and why we were prepared to risk their anger. What more could they do to us?

"One of our demands was that we be allowed to go on the radio four hours each day, two every morning and two at night. And that's what we did, and we were well prepared, too.

"I'm sure you remember listening to your father on the radio. You probably can't recall what he said, you were so young, but he was eloquent. All of the Indians were, men and women both. They had their facts and they told the truth.

"Still, we did not expect to win anything directly either by using the radio or by seizing the leader. The white people had never listened to us before, so why should they now? That is what we thought. And we expected that sooner or later they would decide to kill their own chief, since it would be easier for them to do that than to meet our demands.

"What were our demands? We were asking for sovereignty and land rights for all Indian nations, what was already our legal due. We were asking for the return of all lands taken away in our lifetimes or their replacement. We were asking for either independence or the changing of the constitution so that Indians could elect their own delegates to the national legislative body. And we were asking for money to help repair and develop our homelands.

"But we didn't forget other people either. Several of the forty-nine were part-African, and some were mestizos, mixed people. So we had demands for all of the nonwhite people and for poor people, too. We asked that all of the descendants of the slaves and peasants who had worked for those rich people for three hundred years without pay be given the land they should have had before or money, whichever they wanted. And we asked for the return of lands to the mestizos and other poor people who had been cheated.

"Oh, I tell you, we gave the people a good lesson in history, like they never had before. Of course, the rich didn't want to believe what we were saying, but anyway now they've heard it and they'll never forget!

"What we were asking for was simple justice that any man could agree to—unless that man is rich and powerful and has to give something up! And that is what we were asking them to do, to give up some of their stolen riches. We didn't believe they would ever do this, and, of course, we were right.

"We knew what they had always done to Indians, and we knew how they had turned the slaves loose after freedom with no land or money or jobs or education, how they had never done a thing to make up for all the evils of slavery, and how they had come to hate the very people they had abused.

"So we expected nothing except hate, and we sure got that!

"After a little while the Big Man's palace was completely surrounded by soldiers and police of all kinds, thousands of them. And we knew that beyond them were legislators and mobs calling for our deaths, while most poor people would be too afraid to speak out, except in their own neighborhoods or when no whites were around.

"We had to sleep with one eye open, always expecting an attack. When I was on guard duty I tried to read the minds of the soldiers out there from their looks and movements to figure out if they were being worked up for a charge.

"We took over the kitchen and cooked simple food, feeding our prisoners of war as well as ourselves. We trusted no other cooks but ourselves.

"The Big Man and the other prisoners were terrified at first. I've never seen anyone so afraid as the brave leader of the country. I thought he might have a heart attack, but he didn't, because we took it easy with him.

"Our elders spent long hours with the Big Chief, trying to save his soul, so to speak."

The old man laughed for a time and then went on.

"But he was too hypocritical. Pretty soon he was agreeing with everything and promising all kinds of things, but all of us could see that he was just a red-faced liar trying to save his life.

"He cried sometimes, especially after the first couple of weeks, and we started to feel sorry for him. Not because of his misery but because we just came to see that he was the kind of a man who does not know how to sincerely change.

"We came to see that white politics picks men to be the leader who are of a single type, men who love themselves so much that they cannot understand anything else. So we just gave up on him, except that he did get to listen to our talks on the radio we let him have.

"While we were cooped up in that big mansion, with troops all around, the white legislators were meeting, of course. They were really angry and vowed not to give in to any of our demands. They now had an acting leader, so they had pretty much what they wanted, especially since most of them didn't like the real Big Man anyway.

"The days went by. A lot of them wanted to storm the place, but we fired a shot every so often and spread the rumor that some people might want to see the Big Man dead, whereas we just wanted our demands met and did not want to hurt him.

"As the days and weeks went on everything became more confused. The legislators weren't so angry, and some people began to say, 'Well, maybe the Indians are right after all.' But we just sat it out, expecting only death.

"You might wonder how they lasted so long, Grandson. Well, they built a sweat lodge around one of the fireplaces and sweated and prayed every day. Those who could write also did a lot of that, while others worked on history and what to say over the radio every day, until they finally shut that off.

"After three weeks the government turned off all of the electricity, gas, and water, but the Indians got along all right anyway. We cooked with their expensive furniture and used their own emergency battery lights. We had plenty of food, lots of frozen steaks and top-quality cuts of meat.

"All this time, we figured that sooner or later they would land on the roof or try to sneak in through an underground tunnel or just charge. So we were alert all of the time. Like I said, we didn't think they loved their Big Man anymore than we did, so we expected trouble at any moment.

"Still, for a long time nothing happened. Fear of bad publicity probably kept them in hand. The legislators and the new Big Man made a few concessions, just ones that didn't cost them anything, so we waited to see what would happen.

"We used our radios to tell the soldiers out there that we didn't want to hurt any of them, that we knew that most of them were poor just like us. But we also said that we were prepared to die and that we would shoot to kill if attacked. We asked them to lay down their guns and go home, but they wouldn't even if they had wanted to. Their officers would have shot them or had them arrested."

The grandfather poured another cup of coffee and rolled some beans up into a big tortilla. As he ate his breathing slowed down, and the boy, too, relaxed a little.

"Finally a full month passed, and still the sacrificers would not surrender. The Big Man was almost going crazy, and we had to keep him guarded closely. He wanted to drink liquor, but we had dried him out, since one of the first things we had done was to destroy all of the alcohol in the place, and there was a lot of it there, too.

"Sometimes he screamed and yelled at us, about how much he had done for poor people and so forth, but all we had to do was just to ask him about one thing—such as the life expectancy among the Indians— to shut him up. He really didn't know anything. All he could do was to moan and say, 'Why didn't someone tell me?' My reply was, 'Well, you're the leader. You wanted to be the big shot. You should know about the people you have under you.' He was so sorry about everything, but that was the extent of it. We knew that after he was free, after about two weeks, he would be just like before."

"Did the soldiers ever fake any attacks?" asked the grandson during a break in the story.

"Well, not the soldiers so much. But there were special counterinsurgency teams always out there, and they started checking up on us to see if we were asleep or careless. One night they actually got part way into one wing of the building from the roof, but we shot at them with machine guns and set off a couple of sticks of dynamite. You see, we had that whole place booby-trapped with grenades and dynamite by then.

"They cleared out fast, because they didn't want to see that whole building destroyed. We yelled out to them later that we were prepared to blow up all of the outer rooms in the building in order to make a no-man's-land if they didn't stop fooling around.

"So they kept out of the way after that. They loved that building so!

"Anyway, I want to tell you that your father was a great inspiration to everybody there. After about four weeks the tension was pretty bad. You know, it is hard to be ready to die every day for weeks and weeks! But your father was always reminding people about why they were there, about how their sacrifice was being made for future generations and not just for some immediate gain.

"He was also a good storyteller and singer, making up new songs for them to sing. They had a small drum with them, and it was eerie hearing those songs float out over the soldiers. Everybody out there could understand, hearing those songs—but the Big Man, he got awful tired of that drumbeat!

"As I said, the legislators started making a few changes, but the elders told them, 'It doesn't matter what you do unless you change all of your rotten ways.' They said, 'We are not here to play games. We are here to get justice, or we are here to die. It's up to you which one it will be.'

"And so it dragged on. I used to stare out an upstairs window at the trees, wishing I was out there in the woods somewhere. I could see the birds up there, and then I would get real sad thinking of my life coming to an end. At times like that I would dream that maybe the white people would change and we could all go home to our families. But then I would look down at all those helmets and sigh, knowing the truth.

"Sometimes we would go underneath the building, exploring all those dark tunnels, looking for enemies. We had blown most of the tunnels up to block them off, but we still had to keep an eye on things down there.

"Another thing I should tell you about. After awhile we got worried that they might send fake announcements to us to make us believe that they had changed the laws. But we insisted that only when Indians whom we knew and trusted came to us, only then would we believe what they had to say. So that's the way we got our communications in, and that's how this story of what went went on got out, through Indian messengers.

"Grandson, once I went in myself as a messenger. It was really something going past all of those soldiers and police! Inside, the Big Man's house was a mess. The sacrificers had taken most of the desks, chairs, sofas, and statues to make barricades and were burning the rest for fuel. The artists among them had painted big murals on the walls as well as slogans, and that part looked pretty good.

"The sacrificers were all glad to see me, my son—your father—especially. He said to me, 'Tell my wife and son how much I miss them, how much I want to see them again. I pray for them every day.' Tears came to my eyes and I held him close, but what could I say?

"Anyway, my message was a bad one so far as the government was concerned. But I did have good news about how lots of Indians, mestizos, and others were waking up and backing the demands. Still, this was bad news in a way, too, because we all expected the government to use brutal force to put down any serious challenge. Maybe they would wipe out the sacrificers just to put a stop to the unrest that was starting to develop.

"My visit gave me a chance to carry out letters and messages, and I was pleased to do that, but at the same time I was very sad to go, as if I was leaving part of myself. And I was, you know, my own son and forty-eight other brave Indians being in there.

"Not long after I was there a group of people announced plans for one hundred thousand Indians and mestizos to travel to the capital to camp out there until the government met the demands. It looked as if right-wing mobs would try to stop them. The government mobilized all of its troops and closed the highways all over the country. No one could travel without a pass, and all Indian people were stopped. They were really scared, especially since a lot of white and mestizo students and radicals were upset over conscription and other government policies.

"So the big shots had to make a decision. They either had to give back some land and self-government, or they were going to have a civil war. Either that or they would spend a lot of money using soldiers to put the poor people down. Well, the rich always seem to prefer to spend money on police—it's easier for them than to spend money to help the poor. So that's the path they chose.

"At the Big Man's house the sacrificers could see that the end was coming, since the government needed to get them out of there more than ever. Also the food was finally almost emptied out of the big storage rooms. All of the meat from the refrigerators had long before been removed and smoke-dried in several fireplaces converted to that purpose. But now even the dried meat was almost gone, although rations had been cut way down. The water they had stored was also running low, so they could see the end in sight.

"As the fifth week passed the elders began to discuss how the final days should be spent. They said, 'This Great House is a monument for the white people. Many evil things have been decided here. Some good, too, but mostly evil. Here it was that the leaders decided to wage war against our people. Here it was that the killing of innocent persons was ordered.

"'This building is just a building, and yet it is more than that. It symbolizes the rich people's greed. It is *their Big House.* They will rebuild it, try to restore it exactly the same, but even so we must destroy it now. Maybe it will stand for all of our buildings destroyed by them.'

"So it was decided to blow up the Great House. But what should they do with the Big Man?

"One medicine man said, 'This Big Man is just an ordinary, weak, vain man. He has done some evil things, it is true, but mostly he is just a fool. He is interchangeable with all of their other politicians. One is much like the other. He has taken his orders from the rich, from the generals, from the truly powerful men.

"'Now he is a lonely, broken, frightened man. They don't even want him anymore, because the new Big Man has replaced him perfectly. And they are afraid that we have brainwashed him.'

"The elder paused and laughed, my grandson, at his own joke.

"'As if we could brainwash anyone! We have tried to set him free, but to be free, for a rich white man, is to be insane from their point of view! And he is still sane!

"'And yet it is possible that they are right. Maybe he has changed. I believe we should let him go alive if we can.'

"Another one of the forty-nine said, 'That will be hard to do. I don't believe they want him alive. He is no good to them anymore. Not only that but he is an embarrassment. All that we have revealed about his help to the oil companies, about his strategy to keep the big corporations in control, about his corruption— all of these things have been revealed by us on radio.

"'They don't want him as Big Man anymore, because then they would have to face up to what he represents. They will certainly kill him.'

"And so the forty-nine argued. Generally they agreed that they didn't care to kill any soldiers or police or prisoners. Their purpose was to give their own lives, not to take the lives of others. As one said:

"'Our oppressors have always loved to kill just to kill. They have killed tens of millions here in the Americas. They love guns and killing.

"'We are different. We must not be like them. Never! We have used our guns to fool them into thinking we *are* just like them, but that was necessary for our plans. Now we can show what we are truly like.

"'Our deaths must be an example. An example of another way of living. We will show that people of courage are people who do not *need* to kill!'

"And so, my grandson, it was decided.

"On the forty-ninth day of the occupation, at dusk, the attack began. Huge searchlights were trained on the Great House from all directions, and thousands of troops with masks covering their humanness moved forward in a solid mass under the cover of trees and bushes. Tear gas cannisters began popping in every window, shattering glass and dropping with a thud on the floor.

"Inside your father and others took the Big Man and the other prisoners into a bomb-proof basement. They were told, 'Stay here. You will be safe here—

keep the masks on. Do not leave until the soldiers come. If you live, remember us well. We have never intended to do you harm. Now your life rests in the hands of your own kind.'

"Outside the soldiers and police were tense, ready to charge. But they were waiting, their officers hoping that the tear gas would make the Indians surrender or at least knock them out. The government still didn't want to damage the building too badly.

"The Indians were not waiting, though. In rapid succession they set off one bomb, one charge, after another, blowing up all of the exterior rooms of the mansion. The flames and explosions frightened the soldiers outside and caused them to fall back. They couldn't charge through that!

"The sacrificers gathered in a central area, and there they sang their death songs, painted their bodies, and prayed. An elder asked if any wanted to try for life. 'You are welcome to go,' he said. 'We all know how hard it is to be born and how hard it is to die.' But none left.

"When they were finished singing, they embraced each other, with tears flowing freely. Then they began setting furniture on fire. Very soon the dynamite and grenades went off, and the Big House collapsed on top of them, burying them all.

"As you know, my grandson, all of them died except one, and he died a few weeks later after I had had a chance to talk to him.

"Many, many hours after the explosions, the government's secret police entered the ruins and began looking for bodies. What happened then? Well, the Indian who had lived, although wounded and burned, had managed to crawl down to the basement where the Big Man was. The Indian was in shock and didn't know what to do. It occurred to him that maybe one survivor was needed to tell the story of what had happened, so he crawled down a tunnel to where the rubble allowed him to snake his way along to a good hiding spot.

"From that place he saw the government agents come in to the room where the prisoners were. He told me the Big Man and the others were so happy to see them. They threw off their masks and shouted, 'Thank God, we're safe.'

"Just then the agents lifted their guns up and fired point-blank, round after round. It was true. I saw it. They killed their own Big Man and the others, too.

"Well, Grandson, this Indian stayed hidden in the rubble for several days until he managed to crawl to a place far down the tunnel. There he was captured by soldiers who didn't know what had happened or that he had seen anything.

"He was taken to a prison hospital, where some of us who were in the capital got to see him. He was very agitated and told me to bring an attorney and a medicine man and a judge if I could find one.

"We did our best. We got these people and went back. He swore to everything under oath and told the whole story of what he had seen.

"Well, Grandson, the next day he was dead. Heart failure, they said.

"Anyway, the judge had set up his courtroom, so to speak, in that prison hospital, so we had all that down. But the judge and the attorney never released that information and wouldn't ever talk to us again.

"I was afraid for my own life, so the medicine man and I took off. We traveled secretly out of the capital and went to a neighboring country, where we called a press conference. We let the whole world know the truth.

"That was five years ago, and for most of those

years we have been lying low, waiting for the agents to get us, too. They haven't yet, and that's how I'm able to tell you all of this, my grandson."

The old man stopped for a long time. Then he prayed in the Indian language, low at first, then full-voiced. Finally he turned to the boy.

"Remember always the great sacrifice made by your father and forty-eight others. Their sacrifice is still alive, like a low flame waiting to set off a forest fire. The government has *not* changed, but the hearts of the people have. We all know the truth now.

"Remember also, Grandson, that your father was not a violent man. Our people are not a violent people.

"I myself, you may be sure, have never believed in violence. I still do not.

"But, my grandson, our people have endured the most terrible injustices for more than four and a half centuries.

"Your father's sacrifice was not a violent act in its intention or in its carrying out, but rather an act of a people's self-defense.

"So I leave you with this gift, this story.

"This telling is finished, though the story goes on yet with your life and the lives of all of our people.

"It is done!"

THE LAYING ON OF THE HANDS

THE BLUES THROBBED FROM WALL TO WALL, FROM CEIL-ing to floor. It bounced around objects, surrounding everything with broad ribbons of ecstasy and pain. Charley, with his eyes closed, had sunk into the musical tide and was floating in its depths, listening with his stomach, deep down somewhere in his gut, totally immersed in wave after wave of the all-encompassing sounding sea. The blue water lapped at his edges, came in somehow through his pores, and affected his entire being.

The strange uneasy warm delightful queasy feeling in his midsection spread throughout his body, giving the impression of a coffee high. Racked with the suffering and joy of humankind—of all crying, moaning, laughing creatures—he immersed himself in what he knew was a universal experience and also, at the same time, his own unique ecstasy.

Perhaps he couldn't put it into so many words—words were foreign to him then. But he knew, in a rather mystical way, that although his pain was real, it was also not his pain alone but a universal pain.

Sometimes beads of sweat appeared on his skin. Images of her passed before him, rhythmically ebbing and flowing with the music. Flashes, bits and pieces, of smiles, deep, wondering eyes with eyebrows lifted, soft hair, hands, feminine arms, sensitive lips, the slope of the neck reaching toward breasts, ankles, legs, a whole figure—soft, warming images, which he could actually feel, smell, totally know, coursed through his mind unrestrained, punctuated by phrases, words, a laugh, all rather more dreamed than heard.

Groans or sighs periodically shuddered through his body, reaching even as far as his voice box, forcing out involuntary sounds, which, if recorded, would have unknowingly blended perfectly into the surrounding sound-sea of the blues.

Charley had for many years felt the power of the blues, but now he had plunged into its embrace in a way that is not comprehensible to the mind but is only knowable umbilically. Shaking, rolling, shuddering, gasping, in the embrace of a musical lover whose sounds not only caress, stroke, pinch, and scratch but merge in a kind of congress, a kind of fornication, Charley now had truly—for the first time—become a real student of the blues.

Occasionally jazz songs floated into the blue sea, but since they were mostly based upon the visceral down scale Charley felt no interruption. Light, ephemeral solos with no feeling were bridged by his own mood. He didn't really notice them, or perhaps it is best to say that he shifted them to a different key.

An indeterminate period of time passed until the music changed, now moving in the direction of a kind of "head-trip" jazz that clashed with Charley's emotional space.

He passed outside, moving like a sleepwalker among objects made phantasmic and unknowable by Charley's failure to perceive them. He gave them no structure. He neglected to classify or to sort. He paid them no mind and thus they were forced to exist in an unformed state.

So Charley meandered, giving only enough form to the blur around him to allow us to say that he did, indeed, move.

He managed, somehow, to focus long enough to collapse on a gently rounded hillside of freshly mowed Bermuda grass warmed by the late sun. Quietly, and without direction, his body began to attune itself to the perceptions flowing there—the strong smell of the fresh grass cuttings, the feel of the soft grass with the cool, somewhat damp earth underneath, the warmth of the sun on the other side, a weak breeze making little arcs and curves around him, and various sounds, some coming from below, perhaps, where earthworms, centipedes, slugs, and little grass bugs were traveling about.

The smell of the cut grass was the first thing Charley noticed from among all of the messages he was receiving. The smell bothered him. It was a strong, unpleasant smell that always reminded him of dog feces. And gradually, because of that association, he was impelled to pull himself up from the place where he had been resting in one corner of his mind and reassert control over his body's faculties.

Charley blinked his eyes open, shook his head, and lifted himself up high enough to see where he was. He carefully examined the grass, but noticing only a small spider on one side and a black ant on the other, he soon lay back down, shutting his eyes once more.

Suddenly his mind focused on her. A powerful, tumbling, roaring cascade of images careened through his memory, jarring him as an endless convoy of army trucks must jar the worms living beneath a highway. It was a series of blows as when one boxer has gotten the advantage over another but is not powerful enough to simply knock the adversary down—rights and lefts, and hooks and jabs, and uppercuts one after another in an endless infliction of pain.

Charley thrashed about a little, his blunders, his awkwardness, his lack of sophistication, and, greatest sin of all, his understanding that somehow he wasn't very attractive. He tried to brush that aside, but the possibility that it was true haunted him and made his mind dwell on the hope that somehow she might, at least, feel sorry for him, come to love him out of sympathy, discover his good qualities even though they might be buried beneath a layer of repulsion.

But, no, he wasn't ugly. He told himself that again and again. And yet why did he have so much trouble with girls, and especially with her? Was it just his half-breed-looking face? His occasional pimples and scars? His crooked teeth? His smallish eyes and keen, rough-cut looks?

Or was it just some quirk of character, a shyness or a lack of self-esteem? Charley had tried to reason this all out before. He had known boys, no better looking than him, who were very popular with girls. But something was surely different about them.

Was it that he was too serious, too self-controlled much of the time? Maybe he was just ignorant of women's ways and what they liked to hear, not knowing how to give them compliments or talk about whatever it was they wanted to talk about. He just got all tongue-tied when it came to saying anything romantic.

"Maybe it's money. I don't have enough—and my car is so old. I seem to always have old DeSotos or Chryslers. Maybe I got to save and buy a Ford or a Merc, something that the girls like."

But he realized that he didn't have that kind of money. He had to work to go to college, he had always had to work—since he was ten, at least—and he never had enough to buy the latest clothes or popular cars. Maybe that's it, he thought.

In truth, though, Charley's mind was not rationally examining all of these ideas. It moved rather in spasms or convulsions, or somewhat like a jackrabbit trying to avoid a trio of dogs, running here and there, back and forth, jerkily darting, unable to get to a clear straightaway, desperate and tiring.

She hadn't even known his real name. She had thought it was Charles, but it was really Carlos—Carlos Garcilaso Ross, half Mexican, half white. He remembered back to when the white teachers had renamed him Charles and how he had accepted that, because he didn't want to be something bad in their eyes. And anyway he had always gone to white schools where Mexicans were hated, so "Charley" was a form of protection.

He had got to where he almost hated the "chokes" himself, and even though his mother and maternal relatives spoke Spanish, he had carefully avoided learning any of it.

"She's such a beautiful girl," he thought. "Just being near her makes me feel so good. It's like magic. For a couple of hours a day, a few days a week, I feel like a different person.

"What is it that she does? She talks, she smiles, she looks at you with her big eyes, but she does something else, too.

"She bewitches me—some way. She sends out something I can't see or can't describe in words."

In many ways, he thought, she was like a sorority girl—confident, relaxed, gracious, polished, genteel—knowing how, in just the right way, to make each man feel that he was special. But with the sorority girls it was all fake, or so Charley thought. It didn't seem false with her. It was like she had gone to some private finishing school, or maybe it was the influence of her well-educated parents.

"Anyhow, she is bright, so intelligent—and vivacious, charming—so pretty, too." Oh, Charley was ready to admit that maybe she had a flaw or two, an imperfection perhaps, but if so it wasn't very notice-able, because (at least in his mind) her sheer luster overshadowed any conceivable blemishes.

"Gosh, her mind dazzles me. I've never seen a girl quite like her. She really likes men, has such an easy way of relating.

"And those smiles? Sometimes she opens her eyes so big and lifts her eyebrows up, with her lips formed in a half-smile or a quizzical look. She's extra beautiful then.

"Her eyes are so deep and expressive—they just sparkle with life. And then again sometimes they seem to probe to your very depths when intrigued by some-thing serious you've said.

"I think if anyone was to do her harm I would . . . I guess I would kill 'em . . . or at least beat the hell out of 'em—even though I'm not sure she gives much thought to me."

Charley's mind wandered.

"Here I am, twenty-two years old. . . . 1955. . . . Those years of junior college helped me a little. I got rid of *some* of my ignorance, some of my awkwardness!

"I was scared to transfer to UCLA, but I'm so glad I did! It's only since I met her that I've been chal-lenged, really motivated."

Charley laughed quietly to himself, thinking about what it had taken to awaken him.

It had all started when he and some new acquain-tances had begun having coffee after class. She had joined them. At first Charley didn't say much; he just didn't know how to discuss or analyze all of the sub-jects they explored—art, literature, history, philoso-phy, love, sex, the implications of relativity. He might well have abandoned the group out of sheer back-wardness, except that she was there, never dominating, always considerate, and, best of all, a good listener.

Her talking was marvelous, but it was her listening that really impressed him. It seemed as if she sincerely received every contribution, passing back to the speaker some sort of invisible but potent gift—some kind of laying on of the hands in a spiritual sense, some sort of blessing, as it were. Whatever it was, it was like a song sung for heroes; it made you feel so good—all without words.

Charley wanted desperately to be able to say something profound, to receive that gift, to earn a penetrating, stroking look from those eyes. And thus motivated he read as never before, visited art galleries and museums, went to foreign films, all, of course, squeezed in among classes, work, and sleep.

"If I ever amount to anything, if I get through college and become an educated man, it will be because of her," he confessed.

He reached back, smoothed his dark brown, almost black hair, and focused his mind on her arms and hands. Somehow he loved those arms as if they were separate creatures, so special were they—and her wrists and hands—so expressive, that he sometimes just watched them until he got embarrassed, fearing that she might notice his staring.

"Kindness?" That word came to him. "Yes, she is kind. Everybody feels it. She really cares. All the guys know it.

"Sometimes I hate it. I get so jealous. Why does she have to make every guy feel like a king, like a center of attention?"

The angle of the late afternoon sun made his somewhat brown skin look even darker as he lay still on the grass. The coolness coming up from the earth began to make him uncomfortable, and in an exhausted, rather benumbed state, he stood up, stretched his arms out, and then abruptly brought his hands down his forehead and over the eyes, as if to wipe away the suffering he felt just then.

A few weeks ago Charley might have run around the park, or rolled on the grass, or danced about, or done calisthenics. He hadn't done much of that since high school, but after meeting her he had come alive and often found himself doing boyish things in a kind of spontaneous outpouring of sheer joy at being alive.

Everything—almost everything—had changed for him. His work was easier to do, driving to college was an adventure (anxious as he was to be near her), and foods even tasted better. He was more acute, alert, alive. His music was better—he enjoyed it more and the songs, especially love songs of a certain kind, seemed much more meaningful. The little bars where his sextet usually ended up were not always full of appreciative audiences, but even that had changed.

Something else had happened, too. He had started writing his own music and songs—it was like a form of poetry to him. Of course, it was simple stuff, a mixture of old-line blues and rhythm and blues spiced up with everything from pop to boogie, but it wasn't all that bad either. Charley was getting better on the guitar and, as one of the two singers in the group, he frequently had a chance to get out his feelings with voice as well as torso and hands.

She was responsible for all of that. Not that she knew about it. Charley didn't know how she would react to his being a picker and a shouter, yelling about nonintellectual things such as taking a corpse to the St. James Infirmary or creeping in somebody's window when the lights were down low. Some of the songs they played were deep, of course, but a lot of them were just plain low-down!

Some of Charley's new songs were of a different order, but it was all part of such a different world from hers that he didn't say much about it. The coffee group had discovered that he knew about music and played the guitar, but he let them think it was just for fun.

Charley sat down in a half-empty café and ordered a hamburger and french fries, getting his coffee right away. He lit up a cigarette and watched the smoke coil upward in little irregular circles.

He thought about how he had gradually begun to voice an opinion or two and then finally, two weeks before, he had dived in head first when some rich kid had attacked the Democrats and labor unions and minimum wage laws.

"We ought to do away with these damn socialist programs, you know. Bunch of pinkos trying to make everybody equal.

"Those people out there . . ." and he gestured toward the city, "those people get what they deserve. Why should we have to pay for their stupidity? If a woman gets herself pregnant, we're supposed to feed her. If a guy gets fired, we're supposed to give him 'unemployment,' . . . and those damn labor unions, why they are taking all of the incentive out of business?

"It's always been true, since the beginning of time. The intelligent, the strong, the enterprising—they rise to the top. You can't keep them down. But the poor? No use helping them—they just squander it. They're either dumb or lazy—or maybe they just lie around making babies all day. Brutes, that's what they are, practically animals."

Charley had felt himself getting madder all the time. At first he just looked away and tried to maintain some self-control, but he knew only too well the hardships of the working class to sit silently and passively absorbing the rich boy's verbal punches.

Suddenly Charley's veneer of civility was ripped away by a remark about "wetback Mexicans," and his words poured forth from a secret, until then sealed off, source. His talk was rough. He forgot his cultivated college dialect and street words came out. Not only that, but his very intonations changed and a kind of a half-pachuco pattern emerged without his being able to stop it. Half-submerged Spanish accenting appeared, along with cusswords and a sharp-edged, ironic, bitter tone.

He didn't look at her.

It was as if he was boxing again, fighting some smart-assed white boy who had called him a wop or a greaser. But now his fight was with words and he used them like rocks, hurling them at his enemy.

As he thought back he could see that it wasn't just that the rich boy was a Republican, although that was almost enough. He had always hated Republicans—they had always been the big-shot, hot-snot, hoity-toity kids at his high school. But this guy—this guy was more than that. With his clothes and money and polished style, with his good "all-American" looks, with his knowledge of everything from fine wines to the best shows in Beverly Hills, this guy was out to seduce her. Charley was sure of it. And she was so damn nice to him, too. Couldn't she see through him?

The thing of it was that Charley didn't realize how much he had learned—not only in college but also on the streets, on the job, in the bars. And he used it all.

Everybody else was silent. Just the two of them going at it, with Charley refusing to give up the offensive he had launched. "Listen, man, I'm not rich like you, but, hey, I've had to work all my life and I know what the score is. Have you ever had to work hard? Listen, man, to go to college I have to work at two jobs: I have to drive trucks all around this goddamn city—load, unload, all of it—and then I play music all night on weekends in lousy bars where people like you come to soak up some low-class atmosphere. What the hell do you do, man? Tell me?

"Tell me, man, which is the superior class—parasites who live off of other people's work or who go to college on their old man's money or people who have to pay their own way?"

As the interchange became more intense, the rich boy lost his self-control also and a series of revealing, foul remarks about poor people and Indians spewed into the air.

"These wetbacks are nothing but a bunch of half-breed Indians. They are racially inferior as well as ignorant, dirty, and treacherous. What about their gangs? They kill each other all the time and just strut around with their hair all greased up on top of their heads.

"Just a bunch of 'pee-ons.' Damn Indians. I know what Redskins are like. Standing around at the railroad stations selling junk and looking dumb.

"Inferior people? We conquered them—took all they had. Isn't that proof enough?"

Charley clenched his fists and considered belting him, but he happened to notice her eyes and some impulse made him say, "I want to tell you something, hombre, and listen good. My name isn't really Charley, man. It's Carlos—Carlos Garcilaso Ross—and I am half-Mexican, man. And you know what that means? That means that I'm half-Indian. Yes, a half-breed—that's right, man. A lousy half-breed to you. Where did you think I get my tan, my eyes, my hair?

"Yes, I'm one of your greasers. I'm one of the people you have screwed over. And here, for years, I've been trying to be like you. Well, no more!

"I'm not going to pretend anymore. Half the stuff you people talk about is bullshit. It has no relationship to the real world out there. I don't like your highbrow music and fifty-year-old wine. I don't like your abstract art and cubist square-heads. And I don't like your selfishness and your politics.

"So now you know the real Charley. I sing the lowdown blues and I write gut-bucket songs instead of pretty little sonnets.

"Aw, to hell with it!"

What a contrast with the weeks before. Then he had found himself with an irresistible urge to find any excuse imaginable to be near where she was, to catch a glimpse of her, or to just be in the process of going to where she *might* be. He had taken to walking near her dormitory, to sitting around where she was likely to pass, to thinking up cute things to say if they happened to meet.

He knew he was absurd. He knew he was crazy. But he was enjoying it immensely.

The insanity of love had propelled Charley into a new, sensuous, exhilarating realm where commonplace things were clothed in magical garb. Her magic, her voodoo, her manna, had impregnated everything with meaning—subtle, indescribable, delicious meaning.

He couldn't have explained it. He tried to fathom it, but all he could figure out was that he finally understood what had transfixed human beings for ages. Songs, endless songs, those were Charley's way of putting sense, of putting form, into it. And he sang the whole distance from home to college, from college to home, and all around the city as he drove his trucks.

But those "crazy days" had now gone. Replacing them were days of a different kind of insanity, born from despair and pain. Hope had been replaced by disappointment. Dreams of love had been replaced by self-destructive nightmares of anguish and an endless dissection of failures.

He had made a fool of himself. He had revealed his

proletarian origins, his street language, his rough vulgarity, his common ways of making a living, his frequenting of bars and dives. More than that, he had finally spoken out and had *not* received the magic gift of her listening. No hands had been felt, no blessing.

He hadn't dared to look at her. He had left abruptly. He didn't *know* her reaction, but he imagined the worst.

Anyway he hadn't gone back. Although suffering immensely, and often pulled by a force that drew him toward her, he resisted in his shame and didn't go back. He went to class but he came late, sat in the back, and left immediately.

Charley had his coffee alone, away from the campus.

But in truth there was more than just shame.

He, strangely enough, and even in his suffering, was also proud. Yes, he had a new sense of pride. He was now Carlos, greaser and half-breed, cholo and "choke." He didn't have to hide anymore.

And he knew he had won the argument, too.

Still, though, he had lost her.

Again, the images passed before his mind. She reminded him of his mother in some way—her kindness perhaps, or the shape of her face, or maybe her eyes. She was somewhat darker, though.

She was exotic looking, but yet she reminded him of ancient Egyptian queens, with large expressive eyes, red-brown skins, long curly hair, and Africanness about the nose or mouth. Or of Ethiopian women who looked like Queen Nefertiti, like girls who were half Negro and half Mexican, or like Polynesian girls from some of the islands where a Negroid strain had mixed with something else.

He had always been attracted to brown women, but, aside from his mother, had never known many—especially not of his own age. But she was more than just a brown girl. She was a royal princess, a princess of the house of Thebes, of Tenochtitlán, of Tonga, and of other ancient and rich kingdoms.

She was a daughter of the Mother of Many Names— Yemanhá, Oxum, Isis, Tonantzín, Changing Woman, Kwan-yin.

And she was a philosopher-woman, an educated young lady of the salon, a polished, finely finished, and yet compassionate human being.

Her father was a former president of an elite Negro college in the east. Her mother, also educated, was a refined woman. If she had been in the east she would have gone to a top-notch Negro school, hobnobbing with future leaders of the middleclass intelligentsia or Negro insurance companies. Or she might have gone to an upper-class college in the north with exclusive Negro fraternities and sororities to pave the way for proper marriages.

Carlos knew all of this. He had thought about it as the knowledge of her background had emerged in little bits and pieces over many weeks.

"It's all right. She's unattainable for me. I could never marry her anyway, even if I hadn't lost my cool. Her family is just too cultured and refined. I guess I've known that for a long time."

He had never asked her out on a date. For one thing, he worked almost every night, and anyway he was afraid.

So long as he was just a good friend he was safe, but if he dared to cross that line—dared to seek to become her lover, dared to propose a relationship separate from that of the group—then he would risk rejection.

He would, in fact, be rejected. And the dream would end. Better to have the dream, he had reasoned, than the bitter reality of her kind, fraternal, compassionate, and final "no." She would be very nice, even in rejecting. That would make it worse.

A week or two later Carlos (in spite of his avoiding the usual places) ran into several members of the coffee club. They insisted that he join them, and, taken off guard, he could not find a ready excuse.

From them Carlos learned that the group had broken up and that she no longer stayed around for coffee after class. Desperately he wanted to find out what had happened, but he dared not ask.

The others seemed sorry that things had changed. All of the other guys were white, and he had sometimes been bothered by the way she had related so well to them, as if racial prejudice didn't exist. But she had seemingly been above all that, and Carlos had put it out of his mind. "These whites are okay, liberals," he had thought.

Finally one of the others said, "It's too bad we stopped getting together. You know, we really had some good bull sessions. I miss having her around. She is one smart nigger. Sure surprised me!"

Another said, "Yeah, and would I love to get ahold of her black ass—but she plays hard to get. Couple of guys claim to have screwed her, but I think they're lying. The rich boy Carlos argued with, he tried his damnedest to make her, but she slapped him and got out of his car. That's a fact."

A third said, "You shouldn't talk about her that way. She's a nice person. The only Negro I've ever really talked to. Really pretty and bright for a colored girl—you know, her nose and her lips aren't all that big.

"Yeah, I miss her. It's too bad you could never marry a gal like that. I'd be scared to even take her out on a date, unless it was just to neck somewhere."

Carlos listened as if in a trance. All of an instant the masquerade unfolded before him. The blinders were ripped off.

He saw her dragged in filth. He saw her desecrated. He saw his own mother. He saw himself. Freaks! Educated freaks! Blind fools!

He was the only one who loved her. He alone respected her. The others—fascinated by her, maybe. Intrigued by her, perhaps. But also loathing her, lusting only after her body, wanting only to play liberal away from where the rest of the white world could see.

He choked in his rage. He screamed; a roar seared his throat. Grasping the table with both hands he lifted it high and brought it down heavily upon them. His fingers clamped on chair backs, and these, too, he lifted high and propelled at his enemies. Then, his fists clenched, arms swinging, he shot forward.

Many hours later Carlos awakened to throbbing pain. When he tried to move the ache in his head almost sent him once again into unconsciousness.

Gradually, little by little, moistening his lips, moving very slowly, he raised himself up. The blur around him began to clear. The world stopped spinning.

He saw the red stains on his clothes and felt a bloody mass in his hair. His nose ached and he knew it was broken. One eye was swollen. Then he remembered. The campus cops had come. Asking no questions, they had surrounded him, flailing out with their clubs.

Carlos looked up at the faint light coming through the barred windows. He smiled to himself.

"The masquerade is over," he whispered.

He grinned in spite of the pain in his nose; he grinned to himself, there in the darkness.

Then he saw her. She was smiling at him. She was listening and at last he knew the laying on of the hands, the blessing.

LENDRA

LENDRA SAT BY THE WINDOW DRINKING RICE WINE AND looking at the people passing by along the canal. The scene was so pleasant and the passing crowd so interesting that she momentarily lost track of her thoughts.

The Dutch people fascinated her, but her eyes always automatically focused with an extra degree of intensity on every brown or black person. Racism, New York style, had taught her how to distinguish every racial type, every degree of mixture. The least bit of kinky hair, or just a slight Afro dimension to nose or lips, or an extra-creamy-colored skin and dark hair, or Asian eyes caused her to look more closely—and to classify, sort out, reclassify, and classify again.

"Maybe it's a disease," she thought. "In New York I learned to sort out and rank everybody, to strip them naked, to put them in a niche. This one's black and Indian only, that one's a new mulatto (white mother or father), that one's a three-way mixture, that one's a real black African, and that one's got an Arab look. And then the Puerto Ricans, God, green eyes and Indian faces with bushy Afro hair! Three-way for four hundred years—back and forth, in and out, so hard to unravel. But we could always spot the African part."

She paused to stab at a neglected mushroom with the end of her chopstick. "Boy did we learn well. The ones passing for white—the fools—we caught them in our net, too. Little black fish, you cannot escape!"

Her eyes read over again the writing on her nap-

kin. "Nieuw–China–Restaurant–Chinese–Indische Ge-
rechten," whatever that meant. She couldn't read either the Dutch or the Chinese. "Lord, I hate it, but I'm
a typical damn Yankee—I can't speak any language
but English. Am I just as goddamn arrogant—and
ignorant?" She thought bitterly, "I hate these Dutch—
they speak English. They speak French. They speak
God only knows what. And I hate these Dutch blacks
speaking 'Nederland' and Talkie-Talkie and Papermen-
too or whatever it's called and some of 'em talkin' Engels
to beat all. And stupid me. 'Do you speak English/En-
gulls?' I feel so deprived, cheated. I'm jealous, really.

"But I swear, Dutch I will not learn. I hate it. It
sounds like gargling!"

Her eyes drifted to the water in the canal gently
flowing by and decorated with collections of plastic
and wood caught in eddies here and there. "But hey,
the Dutch aren't like what I thought they would be.
They're pretty damned friendly, good-natured, polite.
Not like a bunch of arrogant descendants of slavers
and imperialists. The women are interesting—most of
'em—with a kind of open way about them. And in-
triguing faces. I'm often seeing some Mongolian or
Indian blood in their eyes and cheekbones—strange
kind of faces for white folks but interesting, I have to
admit.

"And the men—not like the white American male,
that's for sure! Lord, I've never had so many white
men try to catch my eye—not in a dirty, secret way
like New York but just square on, as if I was just another interesting woman.

"And now I've seen so many going with black and
brown and Asian women—just as if this was a natural
thing to do!"

She smiled to herself. "But my mean look freezes
'em fast!"

Lendra finished her wine and silently paid the bill. She left without saying, "Dag." What did it mean to her? "I'm not going to be like those Dutch people, always going 'daaaaa' in that sweet singsong voice and even saying good-bye to people at other tables, people they don't even know! Hey, in New York you'd be put in the crazyhouse for that!"

She paused to glance at herself in a mirror. Her face looked tired and bitter. In spite of the deep brown color of her skin, she thought she could see lines forming where they shouldn't be. "I'm too young for that. Oh, well, what the heck, a few days ago I was ready to die anyway. So what does it matter? Or do I want to live now? Oh, Lord, I'm getting confused!"

Her feet took her over the cut stones and carefully hand-laid bricks, along the canals, and down narrow shopping streets. The feel of the city overcame her and for a time she was happy, happy to be in Holland, happy to be in a place so different from the USA. Here she gradually allowed herself to feel like just another person—maybe from Surinam, or Curaçao, or Cape Verde. She allowed herself to forget her minorityness. All kinds of people passed her, and she paused here and there to look into a Muslim meat market, a Turkish shop, and an Egyptian restaurant.

Lendra finally sat down on a bench and watched houseboats along a quiet side canal. "Woman, I am confused. I can't tell who's who here. These blacks look so damn different. I can't tell who has Hindustani blood, who has Javanese, who has American Indian, or who has a bit of all three. I can't tell the Moluccans from the Surinamers. And the people from Cape Verde, Aruba, and Curaçao, let's face it, my system of sorting just won't do.

"Where do these people come from?"

Finally she got up and made her way along a narrow street to the ethnology museum—the museum for "Volkenkunde." It was on her list of places to investigate, and although she had been to many museums elsewhere, she never grew tired of what was, for her, an adventure in discovery. The employees were quite friendly, which momentarily revived her anger since she didn't want to like the Dutch.

Inside, the many Indonesian exhibits caught her eye, but then she noticed a little bookstore and wandered over that way. She passed over books in Dutch but found a great many in English dealing with American Indians, Africans, and ethnic minorities. What caught her attention were the many pamphlets relating to struggling groups and minorities.

"Typical of the Dutch. That damn Calvinistic social conscience they talk about—collective guilt—to cover up their evil deeds!"

She glanced at a series of museum publications, hoping to find something on slavery or the slave trade. But the only publication that interested her was one on kayaks found in the Netherlands. "What do they mean, kayaks in Holland? Are they trying to take credit away from the Inuit?"

Lendra had read many books about Indians and Inuit, because on her mother's side she was part Native American. "Kayaks have been found in a dozen places in the Netherlands," she read, and the author had traced all of them to Greenland. "So they were made by the Inuit, but how did they get to Europe?" she thought. It turned out that some of them probably were brought back by Dutch whaling ships, but a couple of exceptions really startled her.

She read, "The traditions of the town of Zierikzee state that the place was first founded by a man named Zierik who arrived in a kayak in 849 A.D." Then she saw that the kayak at a town called Hoorn had been navigated into the harbor by a Greenlander, and his skin, along with the kayak, was preserved there. "Wow, and what's this?" She skimmed through the pamphlet rapidly, discovering that an Inuit had paddled into the mouth of the Don River of Scotland in the year 1700 or thereabouts.

"So I've learned that Indians from New York of mama's tribe were brought here to Holland in 1644 by Dutch soldiers, while others were sent to Bermuda and Curaçao. Then lots of Indians from Brazil were brought here at the same time, and some came earlier for education. And Brazilian Indians went to the Gold Coast and Angola with the Dutch in the 1630s to defeat the Portuguese. And the Portuguese took Indians and half-breeds from Brazil to Angola to fight the Dutch. This is a lot to absorb!

"And then there are those Africans who were set free at Middleburg—or was it Vlissingen?—in 1597 I think, because the local magistrate refused to allow them to be sold. And now this guy is telling me that Inuit came to Europe! And that Inuit were in Holland in 1566! And one of those Brazilian half-breeds who came here, to Leiden of all places, married two Dutch women and abandoned them and his quadroon kids to go back to Brazil!

"What does this all mean? The Dutch must have brought back the whole world here, Javanese and Ceylonese probably, too, maybe Chinese and Japanese wives. Who knows? Maybe Egyptians or Turks from the Crusades? No wonder the Dutch don't look quite white—some of them. I always thought the mixing went the other way!"

Lendra wandered through the African and Indian exhibits, noting in spite of herself the nice objects and sympathetic treatment. Eventually she ended up at an exhibit on "four hundred years of Japan-Nederland" something or another. Her eyes were attracted by colorful Japanese paintings showing various kinds of Europeans as curiosities. What struck her very quickly was that not all of the visitors were white; many, in fact, were black or brown. "My God, these are pictures of the Portuguese arriving in Japan in the sixteenth century, and they have lots of Africans and brown people along! They look like sailors, but maybe they're servants—slaves more likely. But wow! Africans in Japan! Nobody every told me about that.

"And here are the Dutch. Look at those servants—Javanese, it says. But some of them don't look Javanese, more like East Indians, Ceylonese, or even American Indians. Wow, almost every picture has Javanese or other nonwhites in it.

"I get it now! Everywhere these damn white bastards went, they took brown people along! That makes sense. I remember reading how Sir Francis Drake dumped his pregnant black mistress from Guatemala in the Moluccas. Wow! It forms a pattern, blacks with Columbus, mulattoes with Drake, and so on and so forth. I never put it all together before. Indians in West Africa—that's right, Paul Cuffee and his relatives went there too. Indians in Europe, Africans in Japan, Africans in Europe . . . jeezus, what a mess!

"I've had the pieces, but I never put 'em together. Columbus took Indians back to Spain. Cartier took 'em to France. I'll bet just about every sea captain replaced his dead sailors with whomever he could hire, shanghai, or grab in every port of the world! And lots of them must have ended up in the ports of Europe. Indians from Mexico in Manila, Indians from Brazil in Macao, blacks everywhere, too. The goddamn greedy slavers, they had to have sailors and servants and soldiers, didn't they?"

Elated and exhausted with her discoveries, discoveries that she still didn't know how to use, Lendra left the museum in a strange state of mind. She wanted to talk with someone, to share her new ideas, to yell out, "That's why they have Indian folktales in Africa and African folktales in the southeastern· U.S. You goddamn fools and liars! You white arrogant fools. You don't even know, do you, how the folks all learned how to smoke tobacco?

"And you don't care, because every time a black or an Indian is mentioned in a diary or a report, you just ignore it, toss it away, and only pay attention to your precious white folks' history!"

Her mind was so transfixed that she forgot to dislike the Dutch and found the narrow streets full of people just right for her mood. She noticed a little coffeehouse and went in, smiling at the girl behind the self-serve counter. Her mood changed, however, when a young Dutch man at a nearby table spoke to her.

"You're from America? I noticed your accent."

"I'm not from America. I'm from the cesspool of racism where your ancestors placed me, and it's called the U S of A! America is the entire land, not just one militaristic country!"

The Dutchman, who looked like a teacher or an older student, appeared puzzled for a moment but then said, "My English is not so good. I didn't understand all of that. Sorry."

Lendra concentrated on her coffee, but she thought to herself, "He doesn't look so bad."

They ate dinner in a vegetarian restaurant housed on the second floor of an old building used as a youth center. Lendra finished her meal, sipped Leeuw Bier, and began to talk.

"Okay, Piet," she said, "I'll tell you why I've got this thing about the Dutch. My mother is mixed Afri-

can and Native American, from the Esopus tribe. My
father—he's dead now—was a brilliant black man destroyed, frustrated and then destroyed, by racism. He
should have been a professor, a scholar, but he was
blocked in everything. But he studied on his own in
the library, you know, and he found out a lot about
black and Third World history.

"He was a militant black man. From him I learned
to hate white racism and despise the Dutch in particular. The Dutch came to symbolize for me the whole
slave system."

"Why the Dutch?" he asked. "I know we did a lot
of bad things, but probably no worse than the English
or the Portuguese."

"Why? Because the Dutch brought the first black
slaves to Virginia—in 1619, I think—and they also en-
slaved my Indian ancestors and took their land away,
cheated them at every turn. So that's why."

"Then why did you choose to come to Holland?
You should have gone to Paris or to nice, neutral Swit-
zerland. Why here?"

"I wanted to find out what kind of people did
these terrible things. I wanted to see for myself places
such as Middleburg, Vlissingen, Amsterdam, and Leiden, places where Calvinistic burghers got rich on human flesh, where they prayed to God and preyed on
Africans. I guess it's kind of like Jews visiting Germany today to try to understand the Holocaust. Do
you understand?"

"And what have you found?" he queried.

"Ah, that's the confusing part! It's hard to see anything left of the slavery days in these places. The people down in Zeeland look like ordinary people—maybe
a little dour but not that bad. Most of 'em don't look
that rich. The same everywhere else. I guess that I'm
beginning to understand the truth."

"Which is?"

"That it is just such 'ordinary' people who become brutes and murderers, especially when they have a religion or a set of values that downgrades other people, people who are different, I mean."

"You are probably right. South Africa proves what we Dutch—and the English—are capable of doing even today under the right conditions of temptation, you know, such as wealth and privilege."

"Anyway, I haven't found the devils I was looking for. No horns visible—or barbed tails!"

"What were you going to do when you found them?"

"What was I going to do? I'm not sure. Maybe something violent. I want revenge! I won't be satisfied until I do something! Maybe expose them in their hypocrisy. I don't know. . . . First, I wanted to find them. Then I would see what to do.

"Don't you understand that it's frustrating to have nations of people commit great evils and then just get off scot-free, with no punishment? Especially when your own people are the victims?"

"Maybe we have been punished. For example, the Germans gave us a taste of our own imperialism in the Second World War. We suffered a lot, although I admit it was for only a few years, not for centuries."

"Maybe what I really want is for your people to acknowledge what they did, to publicly apologize, and to try to make amends."

"I see," responded Piet. "We do try to support many Third World causes, or some of us do anyway. . . . But it is true that we keep quiet about our collective past as exploiters. We don't really apologize for our ancestors, even our recent ones."

She looked around at the youngish Dutch people in the restaurant. They were friendly, "alternative" types. Socially conscious, she thought, probably reformed hippies. Would they have lined up to serve on a slave ship? Would they have become brutish slavemasters in Surinam? "What happened to all of the money?" she asked. "The gold from slavery and from colonialism?"

"I honestly can't say," he responded. "A lot of it was spent to fight wars. Much of it was wasted. A lot of towns went broke when their rivers silted up, and the English took a lot of the colonies away. But, really, I guess some of our museums, universities, and monuments—even churches—all profited from it. I guess we're all guilty in a way. We all enjoyed the sugar, tobacco, and chocolate from Surinam."

"Collective guilt!" she said. "That's an easy answer. But I want to find the truth. I'll just have to keep looking."

"I guess the profits from slavery were used to help finance what we call the Enlightenment and our early capitalism, but it's nicely hidden. Really, I guess our recent exploitation of places such as Indonesia, Surinam, Curaçao, and Aruba is more pertinent. The oil, you see, lots of oil, and raw materials. Maybe the earlier profits from slavery were just lost in wars."

"Yeah, wars over empire! You Europeans are always fighting each other for empire, aren't you? Maybe I should put that in the past tense, but your great ally, the USA, is the big, new empire, so it's all the same."

"You don't like your own country, do you?" he asked.

Lendra smiled, her lips forming a sarcastic answer. But then she said thoughtfully, "I do like the country. I just don't like what the white folks have done to it! For me, it's like living inside a pressure cooker, always boiling and fuming, always on your guard, enemies all around. But I guess you couldn't understand. Europeans always seem so pleased with the Statue of

Liberty and Disneyland! God's paradise for white folks!"

"No, I think I wouldn't understand, but we have people here, the Moluccans, who feel alienated that way. But I can't see things the way they do, even though I'm a quarter Indonesian—my father was half Javanese, but I've always been Dutch. I mean I was, well, born in Nederland, so I don't know what it is like."

"Nobody treats you differently because you're part Asian?"

"No, well, I don't think so. I don't think we are inclined to dwell upon a person's racial ancestry. I mean we have ancestors of many types—Spanish, for example, and before that Norse and Romans, and, well, people have been migrating into Nederland from what is now Germany and Belgium for centuries, since the beginnings, I would think! But things may well change now, since there are more visibly different people here than ever before—or at least since the Roman days or the Spanish wars."

"You mean the Turks, Surinamers, Moroccans?"

"Yes. Who knows what will happen? Maybe we will become open racists like our relations in Zuid Afrika, although I hope not."

"Do you have many nonwhites teaching in your schools, in the universities? And do you teach the history of Surinam, Indonesia, and so on?"

"Not enough. I mean, well, I don't know what the numbers are, but they must be very few. Some students, of course. Most of our subjects are not oriented toward the Third World, mostly just Europe and the United States, and as for employment, we reserve almost all of our jobs for our own white Dutch people. You'll hardly ever see a Surinamer driving a bus or a tram or even working at a store counter. We'd rather have them on welfare!"

Lendra got off the boat train at Liverpool Street Station. Eventually she made her way via the underground to an area of modestly priced bed and breakfasts near Russell Square. The sights, sounds, and smells of London were quite different from those of Holland, and she was secretly pleased. The prosperity and neatness of the Dutch had angered her, while the decay and obvious decline of England made her feel good. "Colonialism's revenge," she thought. "The English are on their last legs. London looks like an antique version of New York, dirty, noisy, and uncared for."

But still, of course, London had a great deal of charm for her. People speaking English made it easier to communicate, and the big red buses, the museums, and the parks couldn't be ignored. Lendra saw many black and brown people, some of the older ones straight out of a Jamaican or an East Indian setting, but others surprisingly English. She went to a Third World book fair and met many nonwhites. Blacks from Africa mingled with West Indians and a scattering of south Asians and whites. She heard poetry read, met African authors, and saw a wide range of nonwhite literature previously unknown to her.

There she met a Nigerian man who came on very strong, "chatting her up." He was well dressed, good looking (although slightly overweight), and very determined. Eventually she agreed to go out to dinner with him. He was charming and the restaurant was expensive. "I'm taking a degree in law," he said, "although I don't really need to. My father is a chief in Nigeria and a member of the government. I could stay here in London living a life of luxury, but I hope to do something useful for my country."

For the first time in months she felt happy. Edward was a rich African, a chief's son, and he was enamored with her. Moreover, he had such beautiful manners and an expensive Alfa Romeo, and he was so insistent. . . .

Lendra sat in an Italian café on Tottenham Court Road listening to Marta, a West Indian, go on and on about black men, and especially Africans, about how unreliable they were, how sexist and exploiting of women. This sounded too much like New York talk, and Lendra didn't believe her. She said, "And what about the English men? Are they so great? I mean they seem like cold fish. You're just angry now, because of your particular experience. My man is okay. Sure, he babies me and tries to be the 'big man,' but, I tell you, I'm enjoying it. For once I've got a rich man and a black man, a real African. So I'm just enjoying it."

"All right, Lendra, so you don't believe me. But you'll learn. You've only been with him a short time. What if he gets tired of you? How many other women does he have? These African men have a low opinion of women, it seems to me. I mean they wine and dine all right, but they don't like independent-thinking women. In the end, he'll smother you and control you completely, or he'll set you aside."

"Marta, not all Nigerians are that way! Oh, I've read some of the novels, too! But they're exaggerated, I'm sure. Besides, I'm tired. I've had a long, hard life already. A rough life! Hard work and plenty of it. It's good to be spoiled and pampered. I'm ready for a little coddling!"

Marta sat quietly for a time and then said, "You're a good-looking woman, Lendra, nice figure, good hair, good nose, and all that. But you're not white and you're not high yellow and you're not Nigerian. These African men fundamentally don't like us West Indians and for the same reasons that they don't get along with black Americans. I'll tell you the truth: I once had a very heated argument with an African, a rich guy also. It was over the fact that his ancestors had sold us—I mean our ancestors—to the white people to be slaves.

"He was drinking and he really let it all out. He said that our ancestors were criminals who would have been executed or kept as slaves in Africa, or that they were captives taken in war who also would have been killed or used as slaves. We were, in short, riffraff to him. We were sold to the whites instead of being punished or killed. They did us a favor by letting us have a chance at life!

"Well, you can imagine what I said back! But the thing is, these chiefs—their ancestors—sold our people to the whites for trinkets and guns so they could have more whores and concubines and palaces, etcetera. You know that! We are mongrels to them, not real Africans, and low-class. That's what really upsets me!"

Lendra exploded in rage. "Marta, I don't want to hear any more. You are a liar! The whites forced them to sell slaves. They either had to sell or be sold! If they didn't cooperate, they'd be wiped out. The same thing happened to Indians, too. Some tribes sold captives from other tribes to get guns. It happened all over the world. Colonialism did that to us. It divided us, and it conquered us. You've been living in Britain too long. You're turning white!"

Lendra's life in London took some strange twists. At first she was meeting more and more people—Africans, West Indians, and an occasional white or Asian—but as she became more involved with Edward, her circle of acquaintances diminished. He very politely discouraged some of her growing friendships, but the basic reason was that he demanded all of her time. He didn't seem to study law very much and instead devoted his time to a small circle of friends and to her.

And he was jealous. At first she didn't mind, but gradually his jealousy began to bother her. He squired her around in a protective, possessive manner and always was at hand whenever she began to talk with another male.

Lendra was used to jealousy in men. But gradually she began to be aware that Edward was not at all sympathetic to the problems of poor people. Oh, it was true that he mouthed pious sentiments from time to time, but in his relations with working-class people of all colors he was equally patronizing and distant. Eventually she realized that Edward was an elitist, behaving exactly like his upper-class English counterparts.

As she became more familiar with postcolonial Africans, and as she read West African novels and magazines, Lendra came to realize that modern Africa had produced a large number of avaricious "new rich" people as materialistic and greedy as the departed Europeans. And some more-radical West Africans whom she met spoke disparagingly of "chiefs" and "chiefs' sons," much to her irritation.

Edward kept promising to take her on a visit to his family in Nigeria. Her first trip to Africa! But it was a disaster, because it never took place. Finally she met one of Edward's sisters in London and was treated so coldly that the truth began to dawn on her. Edward had no intention of taking her to Africa.

Lendra was invited by Marta and a white English friend of Marta's to take a vacation together. They couldn't afford to go far, but it was possible to visit Wales, returning to London by way of Bristol and Cornwall. Lendra decided to go along, because Edward was harassing her daily, alternately pleading and threatening.

It was enlightening to travel with an English woman

and a "Black British." She found that she rather liked Britain after all. Racism there was, but it was so confused with social-class bias that it had a different quality than in the United States. She saw interracial couples and found that people did not automatically categorize her because of color. Money, clothing, and dialect seemed to count for more.

She saw white and black youths gathered together in groups in the inner cities. She saw black girls in tight jeans and high heels dating white boys with punk haircuts. She was reminded of what she had seen in Holland: Surinam boys dancing to disco music along with whites and mixed-bloods right on some main shopping street, with no one giving the situation any negative attention. Her visions of evil, racist Europeans were gradually changing. Oh, she heard of, and saw, problems of discrimination and alienation, but the white working class was also treated badly, or so it seemed to her. Her hatred, her dreams, her preconceptions, were unraveling, but what was the truth? She was homesick and her hard-earned savings were beginning to run low. But somehow she didn't want to leave. There was so much to learn, so many places to go. And her Dutch friend Piet came into her thoughts again. He was easygoing, matter-of-fact, gentle. But he was white in spite of a little Indonesian blood. Where to go? "I didn't even sleep with him," she thought. "He probably has someone else. Anyway, it would never work. But it would be nice to go back to school in Holland or maybe in Britain. I could also try Africa on my own. But then maybe I should try the West Indies. Maybe the secret is there, on Curaçao where some of my kinfolk were taken or on some other island populated by people like me!"

Instead, she flew back to New York. That was the line of least resistance, the familiar and the sensible.

Lendra took the bus from Kennedy Airport into down-town Manhattan. She looked at everything through new eyes. It looked the same and yet alien. As she walked out of the bus station to get a taxi, a sudden panic overwhelmed her. "I'm trapped. I'm going back into the same old world I've always been in. I feel as if I'm choking." Abruptly she took her bags back into the station. Quickly she purchased a ticket for Kennedy and boarded a bus just ready to leave. "I'm not going to stay here to suffocate in this place. I am *real*, not anybody's stereotype! I don't know where I'm going, but I *am* going!"

As the bus turned out into the street an old song came to her silently moving lips: "Before I'll be a slave, I'll be molding in my grave."

THE EDGE OF THINGS

I FELT THE COLD SWEAT ON MY FOREHEAD AND TORE OFF a piece of toilet paper, wiping the sweat away with short, hard strokes. Most of all, though, I felt relief—shivering, beautiful, all-encompassing—the relief that comes from the sudden cessation of pain. It didn't last long but gave me time to read some of the grafitti on the door. Then the nausea began building up again. It reminded me of why I was there, and fear returned, seeping into my cavities, slowly filling them with its substance.

Finally I was able to relax in the safety of that little stall, shut off from the outside world. I lit up a cigarette and, after being sure that I'd got rid of everything, worked up the confidence to leave the men's room.

I still had an hour or so. Looking around for something to do, I saw a sign indicating that there was a cafeteria downstairs. Deciding nervously that I needed to check my notes once again, I went down stairs and around a bend and joined the cafeteria line. It was mostly patronized by secretaries and working-class people. I got my coffee and found a seat off to one side, but there weren't many people there.

My notes soon bored me. I knew it all anyway, so I let my mind wander into passageways whose door had been jarred open by tension.

My mind took me to the top of the Washington Monument. On one side was the White House, on another the Pentagon. I was overwhelmed by the immensity of my task. Who would be so bold, so foolish, as to attack white society right here in its capital city? What was Indian out there? Maybe they were right!

I should just go home.

Transfixed, I waited until everyone else had left the viewing platform. Then just as the elevator was about to disgorge a new group of tourists, I picked up my notes and raced down the stairs.

Suddenly, I was in the Bureau of Indian Affairs building. Then quickly I moved into a large conference room, where I stood in front of an irate mob of white professors and academicians, their faces distorted by ugly grimaces, their fists held menacingly in the air, and their throats giving rise to obscene and hateful declarations. Just then someone started shooting at me. I ducked behind the solid oak podium, my notes flying everywhere.

Lips tightened, eyes narrowed, body hardened, I began firing back with a pistol. The noise was terrible. There were screams and sounds of bullets hitting nearby. Then, in the general turmoil, a woman of color I had seen before somewhere came up to me and said, "C'mon, brother, it's time to go. You gotta get outta here!" As she led me through a maze of rooms, hallways, doors, and alleys, which we passed through in quick succession, she told me, "I'm your mystic twin. At last I've found you. Don't worry. We'll get away or at least die trying. I've got a gun, too." And sure enough she had a submachine gun under her arm. I smiled to myself, knowing that we would either die together or escape together, in either event bringing a beautiful and heroic finish to the whole affair.

The conference was in ruins and all because of one angry Indian and his mystic twin. A broad smile crossed my face as I sat there in the cafeteria imagining the turmoil I had set in motion.

Feeling somewhat elated but also in a rather belligerent, battle-ready mood, I leaned my head back and looked up at the space between me and the ceiling. It was then that I spotted out of the corner of my eye a wild-honey-colored, keen-featured black woman a few tables away. Her undulating black hair was long, probably straightened, I thought to myself. She had been watching me, it seemed, but now she turned away with a rather cold or perhaps merely suspicious glance.

The thing that struck me was how familiar she seemed. True, her face had a rather Indian cast to it, and at first I thought that that was all there was to it—just a reminder of many Indian faces I had loved with eyes, fingers, and lips.

But I grew more uneasy, trying to recall where I had seen that face. Then I remembered—it was the face of my mystic twin, the one in the daydream. But, oh well, I thought, maybe I had just noticed her there without realizing it and put her in my fantasy. Or was there something else? Maybe I had taken her out of my dream and placed her there at that table!

That was it. I sat there looking at her without realizing that I was staring. She was a striking woman, not pretty in a doll-like way. No, but she was handsome, with strong features of the kind that I liked. Had I ever seen her before? Mentally, my hands lightly touched the taut hollows behind her ankles and the more ample brown flesh of her calves.

Eventually she took out a cigarette. Fumbling through her little purse, she looked for a light but couldn't find one. I got up and walked over, offering her one. It was an unusual thing for me to do, and I was nervous as I struck the match and held it out, saying not a word. She sucked in on her cigarette, looked up at me, and exhaled a puff of smoke in my direction.

For some reason I smiled spontaneously at her and sat down. She smiled back also, an unreserved, open smile that surprised and pleased me. I felt as if I was still daydreaming and in that frame of mind addressed her: "Sorry, if I was staring at you. You reminded me of someone."

She smiled and said, "I've heard that before."

"Yeah, I bet that's true—but, well, anyway, you were just in a daydream I was having. Then I noticed you were looking at me. Did I look as if I was out of my head?"

"I was worried about you for a time—so many frowns and mean faces—and then a big smile. What were you doing, having an argument with yourself?" She laughed a little.

I told her a little about my fantasy, but not about the mystic twin part.

"Are you Indian?" she asked and when I nodded yes, she added, "What got you so upset? You tryin' to fight the Man all by yourself? You don't look like you on the warpath, with your suit and tie, all dressed up so fancy."

"It's a long story. In a way, I am in a war but not with guns. A war of words and ideas. I've got to give a speech today—in an hour—and I'm going to say a lot of things that some people won't want to hear. I guess I'm a little tense and upset about that. I may be all alone in front of an audience, probably most of it hostile."

"I get the picture," she responded quietly. For a moment she looked at me somewhat quizzically, with a soft, steady smile. I just smiled back at her, infected by the unusual state of reality created by my tension and excitement.

I said, "You're a very beautiful woman. No, I mean it. I don't say that very often. You seem kind of self-confident and sure, friendly but in control of the situation. Anyway, you *are* beautiful—in a handsome way like an Egyptian queen. I like talking with you, but maybe I'm boring."

"No," she said, putting her hand softly on my arm, "you're not boring. You're pretty good-looking yourself, but there's something else, too. . . . I hope you really tell them something today. What are you going to be talking about?"

"Oh, it's a national scholarly meeting—historians, anthropologists and so on—and I'm going to tell them just what racist, colonialist bastards the majority of them have been. That's all."

She pursed her lips. "I don't know much about anthropology. They don't study black people. We just have sociologists messing around with us!"

"That's just it. That's a good example. Why should anthropologists study Indians and sociologists study black people? They've just staked out territories for themselves. That's all they've done!"

"Are you some kind of professor? You look too young, though."

"I do teach part-time in a college, but I'm still a graduate student, finishing my Ph.D. degree. I may not get to ever complete it, though, because I'm always fighting with some of the professors."

"I been goin' to college part-time in the District here, but I haven't gotten very far. I'm a workin' girl," she said, and laughed.

She took out another cigarette and I struck a match for her. "I've got some things to show you," I said. I got my briefcase and opened it up. In it were several articles I had written. One was a criticism of racist scholarship in North America. Another dealt with prejudice against people of Indian ancestry. Still another was a feeble attempt at a fictionalized account of how the devil had made a deal with a white historian to falsify history by calling the Europeans "Americans" and the Americans "Indians."

She surprised me by glancing through the articles with apparent interest.

I said, "They're for you to have. I wrote them. I'd like you to have them, if you want. . . . As you can see, I'm pretty radical!" I laughed.

"You're mad," she said, "absolutely mad. . . . But then in this society that means that you are sane, truly sane!" She laughed also.

After awhile she touched my hand and spoke softly, "You're very young to write like this. You must be born under a sign. I admire someone like you." She looked very serious at first, but then she smiled with her eyes and I felt deeply touched. Suddenly I said, "Why don't you come with me? Come hear me give my talk. It would mean a lot to me."

She laughed. "They would never let me in! And what would I do among all those professors? No, I'd feel out of place."

"Well," I said, "I would be there with you and you would be with me. So we both would have somebody."

"Which would you rather do—talk to those scholars or make love to me?"

I was taken aback for a minute, just sat there grinning. "I'd like to do both but not at the same time. . . . Listen, a man makes love to a woman in many ways. Making love in the flesh is just one way. He also makes love to her when he does something for her, gives her a part of himself, something important. So if you come to hear me, I'll be . . . do you understand? It sounds crazy to you, doesn't it?"

"I understand."

"What I'm doing is important . . . to me, at least. And for some strange reason I feel that I need you there. You were in my fantasy, so maybe you have to be there."

My eyes were closed. I ran my fingers through her hair, which was soft, very soft to my touch. I smelled her hair carefully, rubbing my nose behind her ear. I wanted to capture that smell, that fragrance, remember it always. And her hair, the touch of it. It was all fluffed out now, wild, standing a little away from her head.

Her body was all curves and hollows as I melted against her backside, fitting myself exactly into her warm brown contours. Her smooth flesh against mine, we were tightly pressed into one shape.

I moved my hand to one of her breasts and gently cupped it, every now and again brushing one finger over the nipple.

"Did you like that?" she asked. "I mean really like it? Am I a good lover?"

"You don't need to ask. I should be the one, but I won't." I laughed. "I made so much noise! I've never been so carried away before! . . . Yeah, I feel good with you."

"Maybe it's not just me. You feel good, because your talk went so well. You're high, man, from all of that. You faced those academics, told them the truth, and pulled it off so well. I'm just the frosting on the cake, so to speak."

"That's not true. You were part of the talk, don't you know? That speech was for you. It was to you. I was talking to you. Your presence was essential. It shaped what I had to say. Magically, like, you pulled phrases right out of my brain like long strands of spaghetti. . . . You know, it takes two to give a talk—the speaker and the hearer. You were my ears!"

"I like that," she whispered.

"Everything is sexual, isn't it? I mean in a way I *was* making love to you—trying to impress you, win your esteem, but more than that. I could feel it in my groin—my loins, as the old books say. I was caressing you, touching you . . . and you were stroking me with your eyes, your smiles, your agitation when I got a good hold on you. Do you know what I mean?"

"Hey, I really do." She turned her head agitatedly toward me a little. "I could feel it in my head and my heart but also in a part of my stomach and in the woman in me. When we got here to your room, I was already excited, ready for you. . . . I had never thought about that kind of thing before. . . . But it's not all that surprising, I guess. I mean, wow! Making love at twenty-five yards!"

"Yeah, like when I was a little boy, showing off for the little girls . . . but deeper, a lot deeper."

As we were walking from the cafeteria to the hotel she asked me pointedly, "What is your object, man? Are you planning to get your kicks by wiping out the professors, you know, throwing things at them? Or are you going to try to convince them, win them over, change their minds? Are you going to just throw it all in their faces, all of their old crap, and make them eat it, or are you going to bake it into a nice little cake, with little raisins on it and frosting, so they don't realize it's their own shit they're swallowing?"

I looked at her sideways, puzzled, interested.

She continued, "A lot of blacks, you know, just love to get up and rave against the ofays, make them mad. But I wonder, does it do any good? I mean the guy feels real good, you know, when he's through. For him it's a kind of therapy, like punching somebody. But, hey, there are other styles, too, more clever you know. Are you clever? Or just pissed?"

I didn't answer—just looked straight ahead, absorbed in self-examination.

She said, "I guess I'm saying, do you want to just slug somebody, or do you want to do some good? It's like I have to ask myself when I'm with someone I care about—do I just want something from him? Or do I give him something, maybe more than what he expects to get? If I give him something extra, then I feel better."

Then, as we entered the lobby, she whispered to me, "Think about it—but whatever you do, I'm here with you." In deep feeling, without thinking, I put my arm around her shoulder and squeezed hard. She put her arm around my waist and, together, close that way, we walked into a conference room filling up already with academics.

As I sat behind the table reserved for speakers my spirit soared. She was a magnificent woman mentally and physically. Just the sweep, the arc, from her breasts to her behind was enough to melt a glacier . . . and it made me feel extra good to know that I could have her with me, walk in with her arm in arm, while most of the white men in the audience could only dream about her or sneak off behind closed doors with someone like her . . . or sleep with someone of her color and shape while doing "fieldwork" in some faraway, strange land.

But from that warmth, that glow of pride, and, probably, that false vanity my mind soon turned to the battle ahead. She was right. It was better to be clever than dumb, better to be useful than egocentric, better to be long-visioned than short-sighted.

I forgot about my notes and turned my thoughts to spiritual things, to the Creator. I asked for guidance and, especially, for help. I decided to leave my talk in the hands of the Mystery that had already assumed flesh in the form of a woman, there, that day.

Maybe men are made of flesh and blood, cells and molecules, I thought, but women are souls that only assume the outward shape of physical beings. I laughed to myself to think that the Creator could have such a good time dreaming up such beautiful, strong, enticing visions and designing them, male and female, so as to fit together, exactly.

I laughed to myself. "Religion, women, sex . . . they're all related," I mused. Such thoughts, and many others, flashed across my screen, played hide-and-seek in my mind, as I listened to other speakers. I felt good, so good, ready to go, unleashed, free, eager!

I saw those professors out there twenty, maybe forty, years later. All dead, I saw them, or old and senile. I felt myself, too, as an old man very soon. I saw their headstones, ashes being dumped into pots with a shovel in some mortuary.

Death helped me. It steeled me, disciplined me to say worthwhile things. I might be killed by a car leaving that hotel; or some old professor might die of a heart attack in the bar out there, I thought . . . or in the elevator later that night. So death helped me, touched me, too, and sharpened my instincts. I didn't drive it away but played with it, as a friend, as a senior professor giving me good advice. I listened carefully.

In the hotel coffee shop we sat down, she and I, for a little while with a couple of my listeners. They were excited by what I had said. It had touched them somehow. We, she and I, were glowing together. I could feel her, not only her body through her garments but also the heat being radiated by her mind, by something inside. And even while we talked with the others we were already connected, fornicating, I was inside her, moving back and forth and she was smiling, her eyes telling me things untranslatable to any other languages.

Aroused, erect again, I began to stroke her behind, kissing her hair, ears, cheeks, eyes, nose, then lips. She turned toward me and we loved again.

When I got up to the podium I didn't know what would come out. The World Mystery was in charge, although the scholars didn't know such a thing could happen. Or was she in charge? It's the same, I guess.

I began to pray in my own language. It was good. Why should I have to start something important in the academic white way with no thanks given? With no help asked for?

And then I sketched it all out for them. I honed away from my speech all that was brittle, rough, and jagged. I sang a song for them—not literally, but it flowed like a song, like a new forty-nine song that you can compose on the spot when you're really feeling it. And it soothed them, made them eager to bite my bait, to take my hook, and even to jump to catch it. I showed how social science in Europe developed and grew up with colonialism, how its very existence and espe- cially its forms were totally dependent upon imperial- ism. My ideas flowed smoothly, inevitably, toward the waterfall. By the time they realized their direction, they were too late. Their frantic rowing could not re- verse the pull. They had to go over the abyss with me.

She took me over the abyss, too. There, in that room, time stood still or maybe sneaked backward to past ages, to earlier lives. I felt the wind of mountain peaks above the swirl of worlds of clouds. I felt lush green valleys beneath my body as the weight of her on top of me pressed us both into the grass, leaving my shape for years in the soft earth to catch rain in little puddles of me.

We ran together along a forest path, past gnarled

tree trunks sprawled about like art objects in a gallery of surprises. Suddenly we stopped, entranced by a fan-shaped bed of broad, fallen, yellow leaves spread out like a bright carpet on the brown forest floor. I wanted to roll about on the leaves, but she pleaded with me to not disturb the pattern, to leave it fixed in my memory forever, to remember us together there. We would then always have each other in the only place where things could remain unchanged.

Around a turn our eyes sought out shining spaces between branches and tangled berry bushes, but the spaces shifted and shimmered as we moved closer. The water of a small run mirrored, for us alone, the weakening December sun and we watched, bound by the threads of many senses, as the shining, curving snake of a creek cast its surface about in undulating patterns of reflection.

I looked for her image but could see only mine, playful bright wavelets of water, ripples, and dancing shadows of leaves forming a mosaic of evanescent patterns on her side of the fickle mirror below.

My reflection looked up at her with love and saw better than I could. It looked but did not possess or seek to possess. It loved but did not crave. It sought to give without attachment.

I looked up at her from the surface of the water and I could see beyond her form. Her soul flowed endlessly outward toward me like waves of sound, sprinkled my surface with bits of her being, dissolving in my stream particles that were her and of her.

My mystic twin—the thought came swimming through my mind like one of those minnows with rainbow colors that can be seen only in a certain kind of light.

My grandfather's spiritual granddaughter, the one

I've been searching for these many years. The one I look for in all of the women whom I love. The other half that keeps me yearning when I'm an old man.

But the man on the bank didn't know any of that, because it was the part of me that could not see her in the way my reflection could. He who was me could feel the bits of her working in, but my mind did not understand or see.

The scholars were confounded by the tapestry that I wove for them. A tight Navajo rug with tough strands of Eurocentrism, with a warp of the epistemology of stereotyping, with fibers of the universal aboriginal, with threads of Bering Strait metaphysics, with cords of colonial collecting of objects and data, with colors of natives for observation and comment, with invisible threads of unwritten tomes about white invaders, with unthinkable bits of strange capitalist orgies and sacrifices, with ignored dyes formed of the blood lust of vigilantes and lynch mobs—a rug, in short, formed of the evident truths of the omission of deeds, of what can be studied, of who can be examined, and of who must remain a mystery.

Many sought to find gaps, to locate holes, in my rug; but unfinished as it had to be, they could not find any. And it was such a geometric tapestry, so Euclidean and Aristotelian, and so gently sewn before their eyes that the majority chose to applaud it and then to hang it on an unseen wall in a seldom-entered part of their minds where its colors of blood and tears could be forgotten.

A few were not afraid to hang the rug in plain sight and they, like I, learned something on that day.

Her smell, her perfume, permeated the room still. I felt that she was there. I could still feel her within me. There was as yet no emptiness, no longing.

We left the conference at the Hilton in a state of

euphoria, her hand in mine. If people looked at us I did not notice. She asked me, "Why do you want to be a professor, anyway?"

"Damned if I know now," I responded after a bit. "I used to think it was a way to learn about Indian people, you know, my own heritage. . . . But now I'm not so sure . . . and besides, maybe I need to study white people instead of Indians.

"Honey, let me ask this: if you were going to be a good scientist, following your own ideas—the ones in your speech—what would you have to learn first? Or do you already know what you need to know?" This last question was accompanied by a smile and a slight squeeze of my hand.

When I didn't answer right away, she pointed to a cab driver, a dark man leaning against his cab just eyeing the passersby. "That man, he's studying to be a scholar, don't you think? Isn't he gathering data every time he hauls senators around or takes some racist john on some interracial womanizing spree? He sees them drunk and sober, arrogant and patronizing. . . . You tell me, baby, who knows the white man's anthropology better than cabbies, whores, shoe shine boys, and . . . bartenders? Maybe they don't know how to write it up or find 'laws' of human behavior, but, shit, they know the laws of the white man's behavior."

I opened the door to the lobby of the Roger Smith Hotel and guided her to the elevator. "My beautiful, intelligent, dear friend," I whispered to her as we ascended, "I have no answers for you, not right now."

It was dark in the room and so quiet. I went to the window and looked down into the alley behind the Roger Smith's kitchen. Cats, big dark cats, were jumping from garbage cans to the pavement. But they weren't cats, just fat European rats fighting over refuse. District rats, federal rats, professors jumping from colony to

colony, fighting over the remains, gorging on the left-
overs from colonialism's feasts.

I had never answered her. Now that she was gone I
tried to form an answer, but none came. I turned again
to thinking only about her, her touch, her smell, her
presence, the truth of her.

The brief time we spent together out in the country
seemed unreal and timeless. We found a place in the
sun and although it was weak, we were warmed by
our memory of its summer.

"I think I'm falling in love with you," I told her.

"Fall in love with me all you want, baby," she whispered, "but let me warn you. I'll warn you, because I
do love you. It's this—love me unselfishly but don't try
to possess me. Don't dream of having me tomorrow;
dream only of me today. This moment is forever so
long as you don't cut it off with tomorrow."

I looked at her silently for a long time trying to
fathom her meaning. "Is it because of another lover?
Is that why I can't think of you tomorrow? Because I
couldn't share you with others?"

"Baby, you don't *have* me to share with anyone.
But, no, it's not because of any of that. It's because
attachments lead to suffering and I don't want to cause
you to suffer; and craving, the desire to possess, leads
to even greater pain, greater sense of loss."

"But why? . . . I'm not afraid to suffer. All love has to
involve suffering. We need suffering to grow deep, just
as the trees put down roots deeper against strong winds.
and storms. I'm not afraid of that. But, I mean, why
should I fear losing you? Are you going to leave me?"

She kissed me and rubbed her hand through my
hair. "Don't worry so much. You're sneaking into tomorrow and you'll spoil today. It is a nice today, an
elegant today; don't make it go so fast by grabbin' a
day that isn't here yet."

When she left me, there in that hotel room, while I was sleeping, I believe a dream came to me. She kissed me lightly and whispered, "Good-bye, my twin. . . . Don't try to find me outside of yourself."

I grew tired of watching the rats. Turning about I looked at the shape of her body, which, it seemed to me, was still impressed on the soft sheets and in a pattern on the pillow.

THE CAVE

"NIGHT WINDS, STRONG NIGHT WINDS, HEAVY WITH SAND and dust, winds that an hour before had been sixty miles to the north, winds that screeched past obstacles protesting any interference, winds that gave animated life to creosote brush, branches thrashing wildly around me, giving the illusion of armies of strange midnight creatures joining my flight, all this is part of what I can remember of that night.

"Oh, yes, and the consciousness of running in a manner so unusual. You see I was able in the darkness to sense the existence of a dry desert wash. Perhaps I saw it as a lighter band of sand and gravel faintly differentiating itself from the rising land on either side—because of the absence of plants.

"In any case, I started running up the arroyo, slowly at first. But in an instant fear took hold—perhaps the survival instinct in me—and I started running as fast as I could. It was like the sensation of flying, yet I knew vaguely that my feet were touching the ground.

"How can I really describe it to you? The wind was tearing at me from one side, my right, I believe—yes, on the right and a little behind, so that it both blew me over a little and helped carry me forward. I remember I had lost my hair tie and small strands of hair were wrapping themselves around my face, getting in my mouth, and every once in a while I would shake my head to get my face clear.

"It was as if the wind was lifting me, helping me,

too, by covering my tracks, I think. My legs were churning but I wasn't even aware of them. I was breathing hard but steadily, running like a racehorse who has been training for months and finally is in the real thing—tense at first—but then letting it all go, and just as if it were one's nature, moving without thought at a dead run.

"I had no sense of avoiding obstacles. My eyes were sensing things rather than seeing them. My body was quicker than my mind. I guess I just surrendered control, gave up being master, just took a seat as a silent rider being carried forward into an opaque but wildly alive world.

"The strange thing is I felt no exhaustion either. Really, it was a rare experience, fear giving way to near exhilaration, sweat pouring off of me, my lungs feeling as I've never felt them before, my heart pounding—but I knew, yes, I knew that I was a well-oiled machine performing just right. You know, roaring along like an engine in good repair. Working hard but at the same time effortlessly as if it was always intended that I function that way.

"I don't know how far I ran. My only thought was to get as far away as possible. I guess I went maybe ten miles give or take a few, and that's remarkable for me, because my left knee usually gives out after four or five, but not that night. No, that left knee did fine—it didn't signal anything to me, so I just kept churning sand until, all of a sudden, I felt that I should rest a little and see where I was.

"I guess I had sensed a change. The wind was different, not so direct, more of a circular, meandering wind, and I figured that hills or rocks or maybe some other obstacles were now on my right.

"Also the barely visible lightness of the wash had changed, narrowed I think, and I saw that the smoke trees or mesquites and brush were not dancing so wildly and continuously.

"So I slowed to a trot and then a walk. That's when I began to feel the heat of my own body. What a change. You know the feeling—after a hard race the heat almost overwhelms you and breathing becomes harder. I gradually cooled down and as I did I examined my prospects.

"Up to that point I had wanted only one thing— distance between me and them. That was the sum total of my existence for an hour and a half of my life. But then, with that accomplished to a degree, I turned my mind to other things—water, food, a hiding place, especially water.

"But I guess that's not quite true. My instincts had caused me to follow the wash uphill. I'll never know how I knew in the darkness. But somehow I had instinctively chosen to go toward the mountains rather than out into the dry desert flats. So I was thinking of water—that is, my body was looking for water even while I was just a helpless, lost passenger worried about hiding.

"I walked up the arroyo as rapidly as I could, keeping to areas where I could feel gravel under my feet— because I was now thinking about hiding my tracks. I began to sense that the banks along the wash were much higher. I could almost *see* a sort of horizon line, but only when I didn't look directly at it.

"I stopped at what turned out to be a mesquite tree and I groped around until I found a bunch of pods, stuffing them into my pockets for future use. I broke one open and put a sweet seed in my mouth. It tasted too sweet—almost bitter—but I sucked on it anyway, figuring the sugar would be good for me.

"My hope was that I could find water higher up in the canyon. Failing that, I banked on locating some cactus with fruit or at least young leaves.

"I don't know how far I walked—several miles—but I began to get anxious and I started running again, at a slower pace this time. I burned up quite a distance that way even though the sandy bottom slowed me down some.

"Suddenly, without knowing when it happened, I began to realize that I could see high cliffs on either side of me—dark walls with no details visible set off a little from the sky. The night had already passed so quickly, and daylight would soon be coming.

"Now I began to worry more about a hiding place than about food or water. I had to find a place out of the sun and invisible from the air, preferably one that would stay cool.

"I began to hurry again, using my eyes to scan every part of the cliff walls and to peer up side canyons.

"I was getting frantic as the sky got lighter and lighter when all of a sudden I realized that there were clouds up there above the canyon. I hadn't noticed them in the half-light of dawn. That gave me a little more time, more of a chance, and, as I was trotting along, I prayed hard for rain, really hard. I wanted that water so bad; even a flash flood would do.

"I also began looking up at the mountains, when I could see them, looking for trees or green, anything to tell me which branch to follow. I watched for indications of which side canyon drained the north side and which had the biggest watershed. I didn't know where the rain fell the hardest, but I figured the north side would have the most shade.

"It didn't matter much, though, because I was actually guided by the sandy floor and the marks left by the last flash flood.

"Anyway, I finally reached a kind of a little valley or gorge coiled way back in the mountain, a very sandy place with a few mesquites growing along the edges.

Ahead of me was a huge pile of boulders, like part of the mountain had fallen in on top of the canyon. I crawled in under the boulders and began following cracks and fissures, little runways, tunnels, and open breaks, right up the arroyo. I could see where sudden floods surged through these openings, but the boulders were too big for the water to move. It just undermined them, slowly causing them to shift.

"It was nice and cool there. I stopped every so often to breathe easily and to plot out my next course. It smelled kind of dark and ancient under there.

"Finally I came to a place where my nose scented a change. I could smell water or dampness. It was clear as a bell, you know. No mistaking it unless you're hallucinating. I hurried on to the base of a sheer, smooth wall. It was wet with little rivulets of water, just little threads of water running down along continuous paths like fibers in a loosely woven tapestry.

"I put my tongue against that wonderful rock and let the water wet it good. I pressed my whole face against the rock and my hair. In fact I pressed my whole body tightly against that cliff, clothes and all, letting my hair get wet, my face, everything. It felt so cool and good, delicious beyond deliciousness, exquisite beyond all exquisiteness. I just lay there, on that good rock, pressed there, feeling so good, for a long, long time.

"And I prayed. Oh, did I pray, thanking the Great Spirit and the Water Spirits and the Canyon Spirits and the Mountain Spirits—all of them. I was there a long time, just praying and drinking, getting wet everywhere.

"After awhile I let loose and looked around for a good place to lie down. I found a sandy shelf up a little ways above the bottom, a place with several exits so I could climb upward fast if a flash flood came or if I heard any footsteps.

"You know, I thought I would go to sleep right away, but I didn't. I was still too tense, too worked up. So I just lay there and went over everything. As a matter of fact, I wanted to have it all clear in my mind because I needed to make judgments. In other words, my life depended on figuring out my next steps.

"One thing was really in my favor. They didn't know, they couldn't know, just when I had opened the trunk and jumped out of the car. It was so dark, the road was so bumpy, and the car was banging over rocks and ruts. I had let the trunk lid up very gradually and the springs had kept it up by itself. They might have driven for miles without noticing. After all, it was so dark, no moon and no city lights or car lights behind them. If they looked in the mirror or even turned their heads, they would see only darkness anyway. So I felt that if luck was with me, they could have driven for many miles.

"Even if they had gone only a little ways, they would never know how long I had been gone. Where would they look in all that vast dark desert?"

He stopped in the midst of the story and chuckled to himself.

"I threw out their tire tools, their spare tire, and a briefcase—oh, yes, and their spare water can—a mile or two before I jumped out. I was hoping they would have a flat and get stuck out there, too!"

He laughed again, shaking a little.

"Anyway, I gradually began to relax a little. I figured I was pretty safe for a while at least, but just to make sure I got up and crawled back down to where I could find a dead branch with leaves still on it. I used that to sweep away all of my tracks, around the boulders, you see, and I made a fake trail off to one side.

"Just an extra precaution. That's the way I am." He laughed again, to himself more than to any listener.

"Of course, this wasn't necessary. It started to rain up on the mountain later on and most of my tracks were washed out anyhow.

"Well, I went back to my shelter and lay down again, chewing up a lot of mesquite seeds, worms and all. Full of worms, they were, but I figured it was that much more protein, so I just ate away.

"Finally I fell asleep and that's how I passed the rest of that day."

He paused for a long while, looking thoughtfully at the now-cool rocks in the sweatlodge. Everybody noticed that he looked older all of a sudden and very tired. He was thinner than any of them and very brown. His eagle nose was larger, more noticeable because of his lack of flesh, and his prominent cheekbones stood out much like the rear backbones of a half-starved steer. But he was not weak; rather he was tough and wiry, hardened by exposure to the elements, his skin leathery.

George Elk Hair noticed how the man's narrow eyes closed to mere slits as he sat there thinking. Finally he looked up, opened his eyes a notch wider, and went on with his story.

"I had a lot of time to think there in that canyon. A lot of time. I decided that it was a good time to fast and pray. Maybe I had been kidnapped for a deeper reason, not just so I could be killed or whatever they were going to do, but so that I could meet the Creator and learn something. So I took that attitude, keeping my mind on holy thoughts and asking for help. I didn't fast completely, because I knew that if I got really weak there wouldn't be any people around with a good thick broth to bring me back, so I just ate little things that I could find, just enough seeds and beans and cactus buds to keep me going.

"I didn't kill anything either, not for a long time. I didn't feel like hunting, because I was being hunted and I could really identify with all the living things, even the grasshoppers and moths, there in that desert. I just let them be and I believe they all helped me, each in its own way.

"After awhile, when I felt safer, I started exploring that whole mountain area. I would get up just before daylight and hike around and then hike in the evenings, too. During the heat of the day I would find a big rock to crawl under or, way up on top, a tree or big bush to shade me. I spent many nights clear up on top of the highest point, praying and watching the stars, and that's where I had my vision.

"That was a big mountain up there, very rough and craggy. I know I could recognize it still if ever I could get near it again."

He stopped talking for a time, scratching his cheek with the fingers of his left hand and then wiping moisture from above his mouth.

"I still remember what I said up there. I told the spirits my whole story. I said, 'My name is John Wildcat. Grandfather and Spirits of the Four Directions, you probably know how I came to be here better than I do, but I will explain it so you will know what I want.

"'The FBI kidnapped me or maybe the CIA, too—I don't know. The government didn't like what I was doing. They didn't like what I was saying to Indian people, what I was writing. They didn't like the documents I had found showing how they had been plotting to destroy all of our movements and cheat us out of our lands and resources.

"'They have killed many of our people. I think they were going to kill me but I got away. I thank you for that.

"'Why did I get away? Why, Grandfather, am I up here on this mountain praying? I believe that there must be a reason for my life, why I am still alive— what is it? I am here to find that out.

"'More than that, Grandfather, I am here to get your help. What am I to do? How can I help my people better? We are so few, so outnumbered, so oppressed—what can we do?

"'I don't want anything for myself. I am glad to be alive. I want to see the people I love again; that's true. I can't help that. I'm human that way. I don't want to hide out forever; that's true, too.

"'But I don't want any riches or fame or that kind of thing. What can I do, Grandfather?'"

He looked around at the circle of Indian faces, all intent upon him.

"You know, it's funny. When those FBI men, or whoever they were, grabbed me I was getting a good salary; I had a home and all of that. Now look at me. Now I am an exile, a hideaway, flat broke, no way to make a living. Yet the truth is I am richer than ever, because I have my life and I have seen great things.

"The spirits came to me on that mountain. They tempted me, too. A coyote asked me if I wanted to have lots of gold, or to be famous, or to win the love of any woman I wanted. He asked me if I wanted great power to rule events and to get whatever I desired.

"And I could see all of those things. A beautiful woman I once loved and couldn't have. All kinds of things like that."

John Wildcat laughed to himself and everybody smiled.

"Oh, she was very alluring, calling to me so sweetly. But I said no; I already was satisfied with what I had. Besides no love is worthwhile unless it is genuine, that is to say, voluntary, given freely.

"So anyway I turned all that down. Then an eagle came and asked if I wanted wisdom. I said yes if it could be used for the good of the people. The eagle said wisdom would not be wisdom if it could be used otherwise. He then flew around me and landed on my right shoulder, asking me if I was willing to suffer still more to get that wisdom. I said yes.

"Then the eagle said, 'Do not cry out. Do not be afraid. I am going to mark you for other eagles to see.' Then he flew up and came down just back of me, sort of hovering in the air, flapping his big wings so that I could feel the breeze he made. Then he took his talons and drew them down my back, making two sets of lines on my back, cutting the skin."

At this point John turned and showed the others his back briefly. They all could clearly see by the light of the opened flap of the sweatlodge the marks of the eagle, long scars running parallel to each other, three lines on each side.

"It really hurt me but I held my mouth tight and then I must have fallen asleep. I dreamed after that and in my dream I saw a cave on the side of the mountain and I went inside. A fire was burning and old Indians took me in and made me welcome. They said, 'Here in this cave, hidden now for more than four hundred years, are the great books of the Indian race. Here in this cave, sealed off from the white invaders, is the library of the great Nezahualcoyotl of Texcoco, a library so vast that it includes books from both the North and the South, both the East and the West, books of all directions, and from the Center, which is Anahuac.'

"The old Indians, who were holy men or priests, showed me how to read the books. They were in many languages, but all had been translated also into the Aztec language. I could read them all once I learned that tongue, which I did. All this happened in my dreams.

"I woke up days later, it seems, and immediately I went searching for that cave. Since I had already been there in my dream it was easy to find, although no one else could have spotted it; it was hidden so well.

"I lived in that cave for a long time, day after day, week after week, losing track of time. I studied those old books and lived off of pine nuts and dried beans and dried corn I found there. It was waiting for me, it seems.

"Someday I will tell you what was in those books, but it would make such a long story. Now I will just say that they were full of wonderful things that, if known, would make every Indian so proud and change the whole history of the world.

"It makes me so happy to sit here and know that those books, which the white people thought they had destroyed, still exist there in that mountain and that no white people will ever own them.

He stopped and let out a deep sigh. Then smiling he said, "As you can see, it is hard for me to stop, but I must not say too much about the books. That will all come out someday, but for Indians only. I say that because I was given instructions that those books can be printed only in Indian languages, never in European tongues. And no white person can ever go into that cave. That is an absolute rule!

"Anyway, I had a good time, as you can see. For months I didn't notice the passage of time. I was in another world. But finally I knew I would have to leave in order to find a way to get the knowledge in those books out to Indian people. I knew that would be a big job, keeping it all a secret from the whites.

"Hah, if they found out they would rush in and build a museum and bring in tourists, and white professors would get everything. Indian people would be the last in line to learn about their own history, and maybe—most likely—the white governments would suppress it all or let things disappear.

"I also started getting lonely. Suddenly I knew I had to leave, but in what direction should I go? I had to stay hidden. I didn't want to die—can't you see?—with all of this knowledge in my head, knowledge worth so much to our people.

"Anyhow, I knew I had to stay hidden. I couldn't be captured by the government to die or sit around and rot in some prison. With that frame of mind I packed up as much food as I could carry and left the cave, closing it up as it had been before.

"I filled a skin bag with water and set out to the south, traveling by night always. My body was lean, free of all excess flesh, so I could travel great distances, eating a little wet pozole every so often and living off the land. Several places I found magueys ready for cooking, so I made pits and baked them under the ground. At those times I just lay around for a day or two, eating as much of the sweet root as I wanted. Then, too, I found seeds of many kinds and cactus buds. I also ate grasshoppers when I could catch them, apologizing for hurting them.

"In that way I reached the Rio Grande, crossing its broad sandy expanse during the night. Along one side I found a pool of tepid water and, after drinking, I took a bath, my first in many, many months.

"I had hoped to find some Indians in Mexico, but the desert there was all empty of people. As the days passed I became more and more desperate, cutting across country in a southeasterly direction. My feet were tough by then, hard as nails on the bottom, and my skin had turned to leather, but I began growing weaker. I couldn't find any water and that broad desert was almost empty of life. When I saw a grasshopper I would try to sneak up on it, but if it jumped I was the loser. I didn't have the strength to chase it.

"I saw a kangaroo rat once and that little creature

almost killed me, but then it saved me, too. I started running after it in sheer desperation, like a starving lion chasing a fleet-footed deer. I almost caught it at first, but it kept zigging and zagging just beyond my reach. I chased it for a long ways, losing my sense of direction, losing my mind really. Finally I just reeled around and around, feeling sick all over, shaking, losing my vision.

"I thought I was dead, I guess, because I heard singing, many voices singing. It was dark all around, but the moon was out and I could see little bumps on the ground, like round rocks, all about the same shape, and the songs were coming from them. I just lay there in a trance looking and listening, my mouth so dry I couldn't hardly move it.

"As my senses slowly creeped back into awareness I felt something right under my left arm. I knew a song was coming from there, muffled by my arm. I looked closely and saw it was a peyote plant, singing to me to eat it. So I took out my knife and, praying to Father Peyote in thanks, I cut off a little and started chewing it.

"In that way—don't you see?—that little kangaroo rat saved my life. So many wonders in this, our world of magic! That little creature took me right to where the peyote was. It knew that I could be saved that way.

"So it is that the Creator cares for us!

"I stayed in that area for many days and nights, eating peyote and praying. My plan had been to go to the Kickapoo people who live in Coahuila, and I prayed now to be guided to them.

"And that is what happened. A few days to the east I met a Mexican family—really, they were Julime Indians—out gathering peyote. I really scared them at first. I looked so terrible. And I didn't know what language I was talking even, just rambling in Creek,

English, Aztec, or Spanish; I don't know which. Finally, though, they saw my peyote strung around my neck and gave me some water to drink, water mixed with peyote juice like in a tea.

"After calming down I was able to explain to them that I wanted to go see the Kickapoos. They were wonderful people, very, very poor, you know, but good-hearted. After a few days they guided me to a highway and showed me how to go to the Kickapoo settlement, going right along with me to see that I got there safely.

"The Kickapoo elders were glad to hear my story. I stayed with them until they were ready to go up to Oklahoma to visit their relatives. Then they took me along, smuggling me across the border without the government knowing about it.

"Well, you know the rest of the story. I have been meeting in peyote lodges, in sweat ceremonies, in longhouses, with medicine people and elders all over this part of the country. I have been hiding by day and traveling by night, seeking a way to safely do what I have to do.

"I have even gone back to Mexico several times, traveling in the desert to see little groups of Indians here and there and down to Texcoco to see where that great library once was.

"It has been hard. I have been lost many times, but each one could make a separate story. My life seems to hang by a thread, but the Creator keeps that thread so strong that it does not break."

George Elk Hair took advantage of a pause to ask, "Don't you feel the need of a rest? You have been hiding so long. You need to put flesh back on your bones and see your loved ones. Why don't you stay here with us for a time? We will find a way to let your relations know that you are still alive."

Wildcat narrowed his eyes and looked far off, toward the south.

"Ah, yes, that would be so very good. But there is one thing I didn't tell you."

Wildcat paused and breathed heavily for a few moments.

"The cave is there, far to the south, and in that place are things so wonderful as to be beyond all understanding. My life, the thread of my life, now runs only in that direction; all else is gone.

"The government thinks that I am safely dead. I dare not do anything to make a connection with the John Wildcat it was trying to kill.

"I cry sometimes thinking of my woman, my children. I cry for them and for my longing, too, but . . .

"There is another thing I didn't tell you. . . . I already have been back there trying to find that cave and . . . somehow I got turned around—I'm not sure, but the mountain wasn't there, the mountain I was on, I mean. . . . The canyon, I couldn't find the canyon either. . . . I know it's there in the desert somewhere. I know I will find it . . . and yet, it's like a dream; the whole thing is like a dream in which I was dreaming other dreams."

Then he reached around with his hands and gently felt the scars on his own back, gently tracing the sides of his fingers on the marks up and down as far as he could go. A smile creased his face and he said quietly to himself alone, "No, it *was* real. The cave is there still. It is waiting for us Indians . . . and I will find it again and rest on its cool earth floor once more."